Fancy meeting you here . . .

Pickett examined the hook and eye for any sign of tampering, but found the bolts tight. He supposed the hook might possibly be lifted from the outside by means of inserting the blade of a knife between the door and its frame, but found no scratch marks on either door or frame to suggest that such an operation had been attempted.

Heaving a sigh, he dropped to his knees and subjected the lock on this back door to the same inspection he'd given the one in the front—with, alas, as little to show for it. He rose to his feet and dusted off the knees of his breeches, then went to report this lack of progress to the linen-draper's daughter.

He passed through the door into the front of the shop, and froze in his tracks. Miss Robinson was there, just as she'd said she would be, engaged in showing a selection of filmy fabrics to a customer. And not just any customer, but a lady: a golden-haired lady clad in the lusterless gray of half-mourning.

Lady Fieldhurst, or—at least in the eyes of the law—Mrs. John Pickett.

Waiting Game

Another John Pickett Novella

Sheri Cobb South

Chapter 1

In Which John Pickett Receives an Invitation, or Possibly an Order

As the hands of the big clock over his bench inched toward the vertical, magistrate Patrick Colquhoun pushed back his chair and heaved himself to his feet.

"That's it," he announced to the half-dozen men assembled within Number 4 Bow Street, all of whom had spent the last half-hour watching the clock with various degrees of imperfectly concealed impatience. "Mr. Dixon?"

A grizzled man only a few years younger than the magistrate stepped up to the bench in answer to the summons.

"A happy Christmas to you, Dixon," Mr. Colquhoun said, shaking him warmly by the hand.

"Thank you, sir, and the same to you," replied the most senior Runner on the Bow Street force, looking down at the palm of his hand with every appearance of pleasure.

"Mr. Marshall? Mr. Griffin?" One by one, each man

received holiday greetings from the magistrate before taking himself off for home. Soon only two men remained.

"Mr. Foote?"

Mr. Colquhoun shook hands with Mr. Foote, a man in his mid-thirties with straw-coloured hair, cold blue eyes, and a perpetual sneer. "This probably seems a bit paltry to one who just pocketed a tidy thirty pounds for recovering the Blakely jewels, but I daresay you won't despise it."

"No, indeed," Mr. Foote said, his sullen expression lightening somewhat. "I'm sure I'll find a good use for it."

"I don't doubt it. A happy Christmas to you, Mr. Foote."

"Likewise."

Mr. Foote touched a hand to his forelock in acknowledgement and headed for the door, leaving the magistrate alone with a tall young man whose curling brown hair was tied at the nape of his neck in an old-fashioned queue.

"That leaves only you, Mr. Pickett. Happy Christmas."

John Pickett approached the bench and shook hands with his magistrate. Having been forewarned by the reaction of the other Runners, he was not surprised when something small, round, and metallic was pressed into his hand. He was, however, considerably taken aback when he looked down to find a gold coin resting in his palm.

"Sir—"

"But me no buts, Mr. Pickett. It's no more than I gave any of the others, so you need have no scruples in accepting. Now, tell me, what are your plans for tomorrow?"

"Er, well, I—" In fact, he had no plans. There had been a time when, as apprentice to a coal merchant, he had received a new set of clothes on Boxing Day, along with a penny to spend any way he wished—an orange from the fruit sellers in Covent Garden, or perhaps a Punch and Judy show—and before that, on those rare occasions when his father had allowed it, he had joined one of the bands of children traveling from door to door singing carols in the hopes of being rewarded in coin (or perhaps paid to go away and plague someone else, depending on the level of musical talent on display any given year). But by the time these riches were divided amongst the singers, the gleanings were small—too small, in his father's opinion, and therefore a waste of time. Since then, he had never thought about Christmas much. It was something other people celebrated. "That is, I—"

"Just as I suspected," Mr. Colquhoun interrupted. "Why not come and take your mutton with me?"

"You'll want to celebrate with your family," Pickett protested.

"True, but I daresay my Janet can find a crust of bread for you. In any case, she'll see you don't go away hungry."

It was too galling, the idea that Mr. Colquhoun might

have issued such an invitation out of pity. "It's very kind of you to offer, Mr. Colquhoun, but if this has anything to do with—with that other business, I can assure you I'm quite all right."

"I'm pleased to hear it, but why that necessitates your eating your Christmas dinner alone quite escapes me."

Pickett glanced at Mr. Foote—who appeared to have slowed his progress toward the door in order to hear their conversation—and lowered his voice. "And yet you didn't extend such an invitation to any of the others."

"No, because they have all made other plans. Mr. Marshall will want to spend the day with his wife and children, and Mr. Dixon will be having dinner with his daughter and grandchildren. The others all have family, as well."

"Mr. Foote doesn't."

"No, but I daresay he's got some dolly-mop in mind whose hospitality won't go unrewarded. Still, if you prefer to spend your holiday with him—Mr. Foote!"

The magistrate's raised voice halted Mr. Foote on the threshold. "Sir?"

"Sir!" echoed Pickett in a very different tone, his brown eyes widening with something akin to panic.

Mr. Colquhoun regarded Pickett with raised eyebrows and, upon receiving a beseeching look in return, addressed himself to Mr. Foote. "A happy new year to you, Mr. Foote."

"Thank you, sir," Foote said with mingled bewilderment and suspicion, and pulled the door closed behind him.

"We shall expect you at three," the magistrate informed his most junior Runner. "Mind, I don't like to be kept waiting while my dinner grows cold," he added sternly, albeit with a twinkle lurking in his blue eyes.

"Yes, sir," conceded Pickett with a sigh, recognizing a losing battle when he saw one.

Chapter 2

In Which John Pickett Celebrates Christmas

And so it was that, at half past two on Christmas Day, Pickett donned the black tailcoat he usually reserved for court appearances at the Old Bailey—not very festive, perhaps, but it was the best he owned—wrapped a knitted muffler about his neck for protection against the sharp December wind, and set out on foot for the town house that was his magistrate's London residence.

His first impression upon being admitted to the house was the sharp scent of evergreens; his second was the babble of noise that appeared to be coming from the room on his right. As he surrendered his hat, muffler, and gloves to the butler (being careful to place the right glove over the left, the better to conceal the hole in the left thumb), he recognized the source of the fragrant smell. Evergreen boughs were everywhere, from the long garlands twined about the banister of the curving staircase to the ball of greenery tied with red ribbons and hung above the door leading into the room on the right. This last he had no difficulty recognizing as a kissing ball: when he was seventeen years old and apprenticed to a coal merchant, his master's pretty and flirtatious daughter had been relentless in her attempts to catch him underneath a similar ornament fixed over the parlour door—not that he had put up much of a struggle, as he recalled.

But although he had only glimpsed them at second-hand, he could not remember Christmases at the Grangers' house ever being so—well, so *loud*. Then the butler led him to the doorway adorned with the kissing ball, and the reason for the din became immediately apparent: more than a dozen people were squeezed into what appeared to be a drawing room. Four men were engrossed in a lively card game at a small table in one corner of the room, while an equal number of ladies sat conversing before the fire. Two of the women held infants on their laps, and when a third rose to exchange a word with one of the card players, it was obvious that one more Colquhoun grandchild would be added to the mix in a matter of months. At least half a dozen older children sprawled on the floor playing at jack-straws, all seemingly united in accusing one of their number of cheating.

"Mr. John Pickett," the butler announced over the din.

Out of the sea of humanity, one familiar face emerged. "Good man!" declared Mr. Colquhoun, setting a tiny girl off his lap so he could rise to shake his guest's hand. "I'm pleased to see you. I'll admit, I more than half expected you to balk at the last minute."

"I wouldn't do that, sir, not when you and Mrs. Colquhoun were expecting me," Pickett protested, his bemused gaze drifting past the magistrate. He had met his magistrate's wife once or twice over the five years since Mr. Colquhoun had brought him to Bow Street, and recognized her now as the plump, matronly lady dandling an infant on her knee. The others were all strangers, however, although one of the card players bore such a striking resemblance to the magistrate that he could only be Mr. Colquhoun's son. The others, Pickett assumed, must be the three Colquhoun daughters, their husbands, and their children. And so *many* children! Pickett had never seen Mr. Colquhoun *en famille* before, and was fascinated by this new and unexpected facet of his magistrate's character.

"Come along, then, and let me introduce you." Raising his voice to be heard over the squabbling jackstraw players, he addressed them in the same tone Pickett had heard him use many times from the bench. "If the lot of you can't stop quarreling, you'll be eating your dinner in the schoolroom and going to bed early." As a guilty silence fell over the younger set, he performed the introductions. "This is my young colleague, Mr. Pickett. John, you'll remember my wife. This is my son, James; my eldest daughter, Isabella, and her husband, Edward; my middle daughter, Mary, and her husband, Arthur; and my young-est daughter, Fanny, and her husband, Robert. As for the children, I can't remember their names half the time myself."

The twinkle in his eye as he made this disclaimer, along with the howl of indignation from the younger set, gave Pickett to understand that Mr. Colquhoun was in fact a doting grandfather. But as he struggled to match couples with the correct spouses, Pickett was more concerned with the adults of the party; it would not do for him to in-advertently offer some insult to his magistrate's family. That they had all been warned in advance about himself and his presence in their midst became clear, for no one seemed even slightly disturbed by the presence of a shab-bily dressed stranger several years their junior. In fact, they were warm in their welcome, and Pickett began to feel almost glad he had allowed himself to be coerced into accepting Mr. Colquhoun's invitation.

His arrival had apparently made the party complete, for as soon as the introductions were finished everyone repaired to the dining room, where they were greeted by the mouthwatering aroma of roast goose. Mrs. Colquhoun directed Pickett to the place at her right, just as if he were the guest of honour, and Mr. Colquhoun carved the bird himself and gave him the first portion. Still, Pickett was very much aware of his status as an outsider. Most of the dinner conversation was beyond his comprehension, much of it apparently referring to old jokes and oft-repeated stories. The bachelor status of the only son appeared to be a favourite topic, and one to which James Colquhoun submitted with resigned good humor.

"After all, you're nearly thirty," chided the woman called Isabella, who seemed to feel her status as the eldest gave her license to manage her younger siblings. "And don't say you can't afford a wife. That excuse won't wash any longer."

"James only recently took a post as private secretary to Viscount Melville," Mrs. Colquhoun explained proudly for Pickett's benefit.

A viscount, Pickett thought, an individual of so lofty a position that it was considered an honour for even a son of the prosperous Mr. Colquhoun to be at his beck and call. And yet he, John Pickett, son of a transported felon and himself a former pickpocket, dared to hope that the widow of just such a personage might stoop to marriage with him! Banishing this unproductive train of thought, he congratulated Mrs. Colquhoun on her son's good fortune, then turned his attention to James Colquhoun's laughing defense of his single state.

"Better to remain single forever than to rush into marriage with the wrong woman," the younger Colquhoun insisted. "Am I not right, Mr. Pickett? You are a fellow bachelor, are you not?"

Thus entreated, Pickett turned crimson. "You—you are quite right, Mr. Colquhoun," he stammered, choosing to address the former question and ignore the latter altogether.

"Oh, call me James, otherwise we shall never keep Papa and me straight," protested the younger Colquhoun. "Besides, we have something in common, you and I. We must unite in our efforts to resist the attempts of our female relations to marry us off."

The three Colquhoun daughters vehemently denied this charge, and Pickett breathed a bit easier, finding himself on more solid ground. "I have no female relations, but I do have a landlady eager to sing the praises of her unmarried niece."

Mr. Colquhoun, no doubt aware of his protégé's ambiguous marital status, pushed back his empty plate and changed the subject. "If we're going to have any snapdragon before the young ones' bedtime, we'd best get started."

Pickett had no idea what snapdragon was, but that it was eagerly anticipated was abundantly clear by the eagerness with which the table was cleared. Even the children helped stack the dirty dishes, which were then removed by the servants.

"A bottle of the '82, Simmons," Mr. Colquhoun instructed the butler. "And you may crack open another for the servants to share."

"Yes, sir," responded the butler, obviously gratified. "Thank you, sir."

He disappeared through the baize door, and re-appeared a few minutes later bearing a dusty bottle of brandy. Behind him, a footman carried a large, shallow bowl. When the footman set it precisely in the middle of the table, Pickett could see that it was filled with raisins. As the butler poured the brandy over the raisins, the gentlemen began removing their coats.

"You'll want to tuck up your sleeves, Mr. Pickett," cautioned Mary's husband, Arthur, a ruddy-faced man of about forty with bushy sidewhiskers. "Four years ago, I managed to set my ruffles on fire, and this lot has never let me forget it."

Pickett was extremely reluctant to remove his black coat. For one thing, it seemed a shocking familiarity to ap-pear in his shirtsleeves before a group of relative strangers, and in mixed company at that; for another, he had no desire to expose his rather threadbare waistcoat. But as even his mentor had taken off his coat and pushed up his sleeves to the elbow, he realized that refusing to par-ticipate would only call undue attention to himself. With a sigh of resignation, he shrugged out of his coat and draped it over the back of his chair, then unbuttoned his shirtsleeves at the wrist and rolled them halfway up his forearms. By the time he had finished, the brandy had been set alight, and the brandy-soaked raisins in the bowl glowed with blue flame.

"May I play this year, Mama? Please, please, *please?*" begged a dark-haired damsel, bouncing up and down in her eagerness to participate.

"Not this time, Janet," Mary answered. "Maybe next year, when you're a wee bit older."

"Patrick has *all* the fun!"

Pickett was somewhat taken aback to hear the child call her grandfather by his Christian name, until he realized she was not speaking of Mr. Colquhoun, but a rather smug-looking lad whose strong family resemblance, combined with his greater height, identified him as her elder brother.

"Patrick is two years older than you," their mother pointed out. "If you can watch without pouting, perhaps he and Papa and Grandpapa will share some of their raisins with you."

By this time, Pickett had deduced that the object of the game was to snatch the raisins from the fire without singeing one's fingers—or, in the case of Mr. Colquhoun's son-in-law Arthur, setting one's clothes on fire. Upon discovering that her grandfather's guest was so benighted as to have never played before, little Janet took it upon herself to advise him.

"The thing is to do it quickly," she informed him, quite as if she were an expert. "If you hesitate, even for a moment, the fire will burn your fingers."

In spite of the debacle of four years earlier, Mary's Arthur snatched a raisin from the flames without mishap, to a smattering of applause as well as a few complaints that there was to be no repeat of the dramatics that had so enlivened the proceedings four years earlier. Fanny, the expectant mother, proved to be too indecisive, reaching a tentative hand toward the bowl only to draw it back when her fingers grew too warm. After three repeats of this process, her siblings jeeringly informed her that she had wasted enough time, and must now yield her turn to someone else. Young Patrick went next, grabbing a raisin from the bowl and popping it into his mouth in a single swift movement before promising his ill-used younger sister that on his next turn he would surrender his trophy to her. At last it was Pickett's turn, and although he had never played the game before, it soon transpired that his years of picking pockets gave him a distinct advantage. To his surprise, he quickly established himself as the most skilled of the group—a position which resulted in his becoming a great favourite of the children when they discovered that he could snatch not only one raisin, but two in the same turn, one of which he bestowed on whomever of the youngsters happened to be closest at hand. This led, not unnaturally, to a silent competition which had ended with one small boy (he rather thought it was Isabella's youngest) taking up a position of strength on Pickett's lap.

"I've always said Mary's son Patrick was the best, but you put him quite to shame," exclaimed Fanny, as Pickett bestowed yet another prize on the child in his lap. "*How*, pray, do you do that?*"

"Best not say, perhaps," Pickett said apologetically, casting a sheepish glance at his mentor.

Eventually the brandy burned down, the last raisin disappeared, and the family returned to the drawing room. But even this simple procedure proved cause for merriment when Isabella caught Pickett beneath the kissing ball and planted a smack on his cheek, to the hilarity of all witnesses and his own blushing embarrassment. Once everyone had assembled in the drawing room, Mr. Colquhoun presented each of his grandchildren with a silver shilling. This appeared to be an annual event, as most of the children had already formed decided opinions as to what to do with their new wealth. Pickett, observing the proceedings with a reminiscent smile, was reminded of his days as a collier's apprentice and Mr. Colquhoun's habit of giving him a penny whenever he delivered coal to the magistrate's court at Bow Street. Delighted as they were with their grandfather's gift, Pickett suspected these privileged children could not begin to imagine the depth of gratitude he'd felt to be given a coin of only a fraction of its value.

While Mr. Colquhoun took care of the children, his wife gave each of her sons-in-law a pair of knitted wool gloves. Great was Pickett's consternation when she presented the last pair to him.

"I haven't—I didn't bring anything," he confessed to his hostess.

"And how could you, when you didn't know until yesterday that you would be joining us?" she responded, pressing the gift upon him.

Realizing that further protests would be impolite (and acknowledging his own need, given the hole in the thumb of his own gloves), Pickett allowed himself to be persuaded to accept. Unfortunately, the exchange had attracted the notice of several of the others.

"But Grannie, those gloves belong to—"

Whatever the lad would have said was stifled as his fond mother clapped a hand over his mouth.

"Yes, little Adam is quite right," Mrs. Colquhoun told Pickett. "This pair was meant for his Uncle James. But I may make my son a pair any time, while we have you with us for this one day only."

Pickett smiled up at her, grateful for her honesty. "In

that case I owe thanks to James as well as to you. But did you say you made them?"

"My dear Mr. Pickett, every good Scotswoman can knit!"

"Everyone except Fanny," put in that lady's husband, to hoots of laughter and the maligned Fanny's indignation.

At last Isabella nudged her husband and pointed toward their youngest, the little lad who had claimed Pickett's lap during snapdragon, now fast asleep on the carpet in spite of the noise generated by his older siblings and cousins. The Colquhoun ladies rose as one, declaring the need to see the children put to bed. Pickett, recognizing his cue, followed suit.

"I'd best be going, too," he said, "I'll have to be back at Bow Street in the morning. My employer, as you may know, is a harsh taskmaster," he added, feeling on sufficiently solid ground with the family to make a joke at their patriarch's expense.

He was not disappointed. Isabella chided her father for his cruelty to poor Mr. Pickett, with whom (she said) she had fallen quite madly in love, and both Mary and Fanny insisted that their father invite him to dinner again very soon.

Ironically, having been hesitant to accept the invitation, Pickett now found himself reluctant to leave. But duty beckoned, and so he thanked Mrs. Colquhoun for her hospitality, shook hands with his magistrate, and, after reclaiming his hat, muffler, and gloves from the butler, stepped out of the warm and well-lit house into the cold December night. It seemed strangely quiet outside after the cheerful din of the Colquhouns' Christmas celebration, and while it was certainly more peaceful, he did not anticipate with any eagerness his return to the dark and lonely flat in Drury Lane. In truth, a few hours spent with his magistrate's large and lively family had left him longing for things he'd never even known existed. At that moment he craved nothing so much as an evergreen-bedecked home of his own—not two shabbily furnished rooms over a chandler's shop, but a house, certainly not so grand a house as Mr. Colquhoun's, but something—something—

Something to which he would not be ashamed to bring a bride. And if he were honest, the bride of his rosy imaginings bore a striking resemblance to Lady Fieldhurst. He heaved a sigh of frustration, suddenly impatient for the same annulment hearing he'd spent the last month dreading. The sooner the thing was done, the sooner he would stop hoping for things that could never be.

Chapter 3

In Which Is Seen More Private Celebrations

Silence fell over the Colquhoun household, all the children having either departed for their London homes with their parents or, in the case of those visiting from Scotland, been tucked away upstairs in the nursery beneath the attic. Alone with his wife, Mr. Colquhoun removed a half-empty mug of wassail from her hand and set it down on the nearest available surface.

"Leave it, Janet," he said. "You have servants for that."

"Yes, I do," she responded, regarding him with a baleful eye as she picked up the mug again. "And what use you think they'll be after you gave them a bottle of the best brandy is a mystery to me."

He chuckled. "Aye, well, it's Christmas. They're entitled to a bit of celebrating, too. Besides, once the bottle is divided amongst all the staff, no one will have enough to get thoroughly disguised, just pleasantly elevated."

"It's kind you are to think of them, my love. Just as it was kind of you to invite young Mr. Pickett to join us for Christmas dinner."

"He's a good lad. I just hated to think of him all alone on Christmas. I only hope I didn't throw your numbers off, inviting him at the last minute."

"Nonsense! What do numbers matter at a family dinner?"

"True, but Mr. Pickett is not family. Speaking of which, I suppose you'd better apologize to James for depriving him of his gloves."

"Gloves!" scoffed Mrs. Colquhoun with uncharacteristic vehemence. "What that young man needs is a wife!"

"Now, don't you start in on him too! Poor James has enough to bear with his sisters trying to marry him off."

"Well, I don't say they aren't right, although Isabella might find her brother more open to her advice if she were to dispense it with a lighter hand. But I wasn't talking about James. I meant your Mr. Pickett."

"Oh. Well, he's got a wife. Therein lies the problem."

Her eyes grew round with surprise. "He's married? To whom, pray?"

"You wouldn't believe me if I told you."

Naturally, this assertion did nothing to diminish her curiosity, and so Mr. Colquhoun was obliged to remind her of his recent trip to Scotland in the company of his youngest Runner, and to explain how it had resulted in Mr. Pickett's being bound in a Scottish marriage by declaration with Lady Fieldhurst, widow of the late viscount.

"Married to a viscountess!" exclaimed Mrs. Colquhoun at the end of this narrative. "What do they intend to do?"

"Her ladyship is seeking an annulment, although it has yet to come before the ecclesiastical court."

Not for nothing was Janet Colquhoun married to a magistrate. "An annulment, you say? On what grounds? They are both of legal age, and I can't see how fraud would be a valid claim in this case."

"No. The only possibility that even remotely applies is impotence."

"Oh dear, what a pity! His, or hers?"

"Between you and me and the lamppost, it's neither. But since her ladyship has been married before—during which time her husband must surely have filed his own complaint based on such a condition—and Mr. Pickett can offer no proof to the contrary, the burden falls on him."

" 'No proof to the contrary,' " she echoed thoughtfully. "Do you mean—?"

He nodded. "Precisely. Although he assures me that he has no reason to believe he couldn't, the situation has never come up." He frowned at his own last words. "If you will pardon the unintentional pun."

Mrs. Colquhoun, however, had no interest in puns, intentional or otherwise, for a new thought had occurred to her. "My love, do you suppose our James is still a—"

"I don't know, and I beg you not to ask him," he interrupted hastily.

"No, of course I won't. I only wondered—mothers do, you know. But it seems to me that Mr. Pickett must love this lady very much, to make such a sacrifice for her sake."

The magistrate sighed. "I'm afraid you're right, my dear. He has been besotted with her from the first, but I had thought that once it was clear she would not stand trial for her husband's murder, he would recognize the hopelessness of such an attachment, and fix his interest on a more attainable object. It appears I was wrong, however. If anything, he's in a worse case now than he was before."

"And Lady Fieldhurst? What are her sentiments, do you know?"

"Does it matter? Even if she loved him desperately, such a match would be impossible. Only imagine if our James's employer were to die, and James wed his widow."

Her bosom swelled in maternal indignation. "I'm sure our James is good enough for anyone!"

"*You* know that, and *I* know that, but try telling the *beau monde* that, and see what reaction you get! And our James is connected, albeit distantly, to Sir James Colquhoun of Luss. John Pickett, on the other hand, is the son of a transported felon, and God only knows what other bad apples one might shake out of his family tree. Any such marriage would be social suicide, and her ladyship is wise enough in the ways of her world to know it. Still, this annulment business is weighing heavily on the lad's mind. That's why I didn't want to leave him alone on Christmas Day to dwell on it."

As he passed through the drawing room door, she slipped her hand into his arm and stopped him directly beneath the kissing ball and lifted her face expectantly. "You're a good man, Patrick Colquhoun. A happy Christmas to you."

Nothing loth, he bent and kissed her lips. "And to you, my dear."

* * *

Meanwhile, in nearby Mayfair, Lord Rupert Latham knocked on the door of a tall, narrow house in Curzon Street. Since he was a frequent visitor, he was admitted by the butler and shown at once into the drawing room, where he gazed about the elegantly appointed chamber with an air of marked disapproval.

"What, no evergreens in honor of the season?" he chided the mistress of the house, a fair-haired beauty who sat on the straw-colored sofa with a book in her hand. "I confess, I came calling with no other purpose than the hope of catching you beneath the kissing ball."

"Then I fear you are doomed to disappointment," replied Julia, Lady Fieldhurst, laying aside her book as she rose to greet him. "You forget that I am still in mourning."

"In letter, if not in spirit," he agreed. "Fortunately, our festivities need not be hampered by the lack of botanical display."

He took her in his arms and would have kissed her, had she not turned her head at the last minute, leaving him with nothing but a mouthful of golden hair.

"Don't, Rupert."

He raised his head, but his arms tightened about her waist. "Why the devil not?"

"I told you—"

"You told me a great piece of nonsense about being in mourning for a husband you were perfectly willing to cuckold eight months ago, when he was still alive." His eyes narrowed in sudden suspicion. "And yet I have a feeling your reluctance has less to do with your deceased husband than it does with your living one."

"And why shouldn't it? After all, it seems wrong for me to—to indulge in pleasures that are denied him."

"He can't miss what he never had, while I—" He bent his head again, this time pressing his lips to her ear. "I have been waiting for eight long months."

She put her hands to his chest, holding him at arm's

length until he took the hint and released her. "I'm afraid you're going to be waiting longer than that."

"I see," he said, glowering at her. "You intend to keep me dangling until the annulment is granted."

"If you must know, it's worse than that. It was a mistake, Rupert. I'd quarreled with Frederick, and then had too much champagne, and—and I made a mistake. In a way, I'm grateful to Frederick for preventing me from following through with it."

"I see," he said again. "Then we are to be, as they say, 'just friends.' But I warn you, Julia, I do not give up easily. I trust you will permit me to hope?"

She sighed. "I suppose I can't stop you, but you may be sure I shall do nothing to encourage you."

"Your very existence encourages me. I shall not say goodbye, then, but *au revoir*."

He raised her hand to his lips with an air of exaggerated gallantry, and she reluctantly allowed this familiarity; it seemed the quickest way to be rid of him. After he had gone, she returned to the sofa and picked up her book, but found she had no more interest in the convoluted tale of a well-born (and, if the truth were told, rather vapid) young lady who falls in love with a stable lad who turns out to be the lost heir to a tiny, and entirely fabricated, European kingdom. Really, Julia thought, eyeing the gilt-edged, calf-bound volume with disfavor, authors ought not to write such drivel. It only encouraged impressionable young women to yearn after wholly ineligible men.

This observation led, not unnaturally, to thoughts of her own wholly ineligible man, Bow Street Runner John Pickett, twenty-four years old and, at least in the eyes of the law, her husband. There had been no word from her solicitor as to when their annulment would come before the ecclesiastical court, but this was not entirely unexpected: Mr. Crumpton had cautioned them that it might take several months, and no attempts by the current Lord Fieldhurst to grease the wheels of justice had had the least effect in speeding the process along. In truth, she was not quite certain whether to be sorry or glad. Given the humiliation that the process demanded of poor Mr. Pickett, it would surely be kinder to have it over and done with as quickly as possible, so they could both put the unfortunate episode behind them. And yet she could not shake the feeling that there remained some unfinished business between herself and Mr. Pickett—and that it would remain unfinished regardless of what the law had to say as to their marital status.

It was with considerable relief that she heard the strains of "God Rest Ye Merry, Gentlemen" being inexpertly performed just outside her door. She heard the butler's footsteps crossing the hall, and called out to forestall him.

"Never mind, Rogers, I'll go."

She opened the door and found half a dozen children of varying ages and heights, all belting out the old carol with gusto, if not skill. Nevertheless, this was the season when intention, rather than execution, should be rewarded. She leaned against the doorframe, hugging her arms about herself for warmth, and listened, smiling, until the final "tidings of comfort and joy." Fortunately, she had anticipated such holiday visitors, and the excellent Rogers had prepared for this eventuality by placing a small bowl of pennies on the piecrust table next to the door. As the last note faded, she reached into the bowl, grabbed a handful of coins, and tossed it into the group. The makeshift choir broke up at once, the children scrambling after pennies with squeals of delight that were only slightly less musical than their singing had been. Having retrieved the last of the coins, they shrieked their thanks before hurrying off toward the next house in quest of further riches.

Alone once more, Julia gazed up at the stars, shining like diamonds in the cold, clear December sky. Her thoughts returned to John Pickett, and she wondered where he was this Christmas, and if he was thinking of her.

"Happy Christmas, Mr. Pickett," she whispered, then stepped inside and closed the door.

Chapter 4

In Which John Pickett Takes On a New Case

The twenty-sixth of December—commonly known as
Boxing Day—being the day on which servants, pensioners,
and other dependents were given their Christmas boxes,
Julia's morning was filled with presenting these gifts and
accepting the thanks of their grateful recipients. Although
her household staff was small, enough pomp and cere-
mony accompanied the procedure that it was past noon by
the time she had leisure to compose an answer to the letter
that had come to her from Somersetshire the day before
Christmas. But compose it she must if it was to be sent out
when mail delivery resumed the next morning, and so she
settled herself at her elegant rosewood writing desk and
reached for her correspondence. She shuffled through
tradesman's bills (one for coal, another for wax candles,
and a third from the greengrocer, all of which must be paid
by the end of the month) until she found the one she
sought: a single sheet of fine vellum addressed in her
mother's spidery script. Her heart sank as she unfolded the
crossed sheet and reread Lady Runyon's melancholy mis-

sive. At least, Julia reflected, she could reply to her mother quite honestly that she had not received the letter until Christmas Eve, much too late to change her plans for the holiday.

In truth, she would have had no desire to spend Christmas at her childhood home even had the letter arrived a full month earlier. The death of her sister Claudia a dozen years earlier still hung over her parents' house like a pall, and Julia could not bear the thought of hearing her mother still bemoaning the loss of her elder daughter after more than a decade. Still less could she face the prospect of being obliged to enact the rôle of the grieving widow. And that her mother would expect nothing less of her, Julia had no doubt. No matter how unsatisfactory the late Lord Fieldhurst might have been in life, Death, in Lady Runyon's opinion, erased all the deceased's faults; only witness the pinnacle of perfection which poor Claudia had achieved in her fond parent's memory.

And, as usual, it was Death that provided the theme of her mother's Christmas correspondence. Beyond the annual complaint about how the Joyous Nativity only served to make her all the more Conscious of her Own Loss, she predicted confidently that, as Painful as her dear Child must find the Holiday Season at present, Time—that Great Healer—must eventually Blunt the Edges of her Sorrow (the privilege of perpetual mourning, it seemed, was one

Lady Runyon reserved for herself), for having just turned twenty-seven, Julia was Too Young to spend the Rest of her Life Alone. Reading these lines, Julia could not help thinking that, if her mother knew she had contracted a second marriage (albeit unintentionally) a scant six months after Lord Fieldhurst's death, Mama would be singing a very different tune.

Still, one of her mother's assertions gave Julia considerable food for thought, and she searched for the intriguing lines to read them again. Yes, here it was, right after the bit about the Blunt Edges of Sorrow. Here her mother pointed out that in four short months (Short? Every one of the previous eight had seemed to last an eternity!), her year of mourning would be completed, and she would be able to Rejoin the World from which she, in her Grief, had Withdrawn. Overwrought though the expression of it might be, Mama's reasoning was quite correct, Julia thought, feeling something akin to hope for the first time in many days. In only a few months, Frederick would have been gone a year, and she would be able to put off her blacks for good. But what would she wear instead? Everything else she owned would be at least a year out of date.

She cast the letter aside and rose to her feet, her mind made up. Her reply to her mother would just have to wait. She would spend the afternoon taking stock of her wardrobe, and tomorrow she would go to the linen-draper's to purchase fabrics for a few new gowns. Not a whole new wardrobe, of course, at least not all at once; the terms of the marriage contract had left her quite comfortably situated, but she hadn't the income at her disposal that she'd once had. Then again, neither did she have the need any longer for the elaborate costumes which had been *de rigueur* for the state dinners and levees she'd been obliged to attend with Frederick. She could well afford a new gown for evening, as well as one or two for day wear.

And as for exactly whom she hoped to impress with this display of finery, well, that was a question best not examined too closely.

* * *

Boxing Day might still be a holiday for the leisured classes, but at the magistrate's court in Bow Street, the term had an entirely different meaning, as those merrymakers who had imbibed too freely the previous evening had been hauled in by the night patrol on charges of brawling, assault, disturbing the peace, or some combination of the three.

"So much for peace on earth and goodwill toward men," Mr. Colquhoun grumbled to Pickett, having dismissed the last of these with a stern warning and a hefty fine. "A pity it never lasts beyond the fourth cup of wassail. That's why my Janet has always imposed a two-cup limit."

Pickett merely smiled at this. It had been clear that at

least one of the gentlemen present had found a way around this restriction, for Fanny's husband, Robert, had been just a bit well-to-live by the time the party had broken up.

"Aye, we're a worthless, good-for-nothing lot," the magistrate said, apparently reading Pickett's thoughts. "Still, I hope Christmas with the Colquhouns was better than spending the holiday alone."

"It was, sir, very much."

"I'm pleased to hear it, for my family will take it very ill if you are not included next year. My granddaughter Janet, Mary's girl, has made up her mind to marry you, just so you can keep her supplied with raisins. I felt it only fair to warn her that by next Christmas your affections might be engaged elsewhere, and that you might even be in a position to celebrate with a family of your own." Seeing the doubtful expression on his protégé's face, the magistrate added bracingly, "Come, John, you're young, and for some reason females seem to find your face appealing. No knowing what the coming year may bring."

Pickett knew very well what the coming year would bring for him: abject humiliation, as a result of which he would have become such a laughingstock that no decent woman would allow him to court her. Not that he would wish to do so in any case, having irrevocably lost his heart to the very lady for whose sake he was prepared to abase himself.

Thankfully, the magistrate did not give him time to dwell on the matter. "But in the meantime, crime never takes a holiday. Sir Archibald Maddox claims his wife's pearls were snatched right off her neck as her ladyship was leaving divine services at St. George's yesterday morning, and requests a Runner to investigate."

Pickett frowned thoughtfully. "They were stolen yesterday, and the theft is only being reported today? Why the delay?"

"I daresay it has something to do with the fact that yesterday was Christmas Day. But perhaps you'd like to put that question to the lady herself." As further incentive, he added, "The pearls belonged to her mother, so they have a sentimental value far in addition to their monetary worth. Lady Maddox is offering a reward of twenty pounds for their safe return. You could find a use for twenty pounds, could you not?"

Pickett opened his mouth to agree, and then hesitated as a new and unwelcome thought occurred to him. "St. George's? The one in Hanover Square?"

Mr. Colquhoun nodded. "Not in the square proper, but very near it—hence the name."

"And St. George's, Hanover Square is the parish church for Mayfair, is it not?"

"Aye, it is," the magistrate affirmed with lowering brow, having a very fair idea of Pickett's thought processes.

"Then—then I thank you for the opportunity, sir, but I think you would do better to send one of the others. Mr. Foote has already solved one such case, so perhaps he would be the best man for this one."

The bushy white eyebrows descended in earnest. "Recovering stolen property hardly constitutes solving a case, Mr. Pickett, and you would do well to remember it! Paying out finders' fees is a far cry from bringing a criminal to justice. I'm sure I need not tell you which one I would prefer."

"No, sir, but you said—you promised me you wouldn't send me to Mayfair, at least not for a while."

"I did, although God only knows what possessed me to do so," Mr. Colquhoun grudgingly agreed. "It's unlikely you would see the woman at all. And even if you did, well, you can't go on avoiding her forever."

Perhaps not, but Pickett intended to try. In fact, it was worse than his mentor knew. If it were only a matter of seeing her again, he would gladly run all the way to Mayfair on the slightest chance of catching a glimpse of her. But the last time they had been together he, not content with nursing a hopeless love in secret, had recklessly declared himself, pouring out his pent-up feelings in a flood of words that, once given vent, refused to be held back. And her response had been . . . nothing.

She'd stood there staring at him, mouth open in shock and dismay, not saying a word. No, he could not face her again. Not after that.

The magistrate's face became slowly suffused with red, a transformation which experience had taught Pickett did not bode well for his cause. Thankfully, before Mr. Colquhoun could favor his protégé with an opinion of that young man's cowardice, stubbornness, and general recalcitrance, the door opened and a red-cheeked lad blew into the magistrate's court along with the winter wind.

"Yes, what do you want?" snapped Mr. Colquhoun with uncharacteristic surliness.

The boy snatched off his frayed knitted cap and tugged at his forelock. "Begging your pardon, your worship, but my master sent me—Mr. Robinson, that is, in Piccadilly. Someone broke into the safe and took all the money."

"Your master is a shopkeeper?" the magistrate asked, moderating his tone.

"Aye, your worship, a linen-draper," the lad said, twisting his cap in his hands.

"Very well, Mr. Pickett here will go with you."

Piccadilly was still a bit closer to Mayfair than Pickett would have liked, as it bordered that aristocratic neighborhood to the south, but he knew better than to argue. As he set out with the boy, he consoled himself with the knowledge that since this crime concerned a merchant rather than the aristocratic class to which Lady Fieldhurst belonged, he was unlikely to encounter her over the course of the investigation.

Fifteen minutes' walk brought them to the establishment of Geo. Robinson, Linen-draper to the Quality since 1668, according to the sign over the door; Pickett could only assume that either the proprietor was extraordinarily long-lived, or else the current Geo. Robinson was only the latest in a long line of linen-drapers to bear the name. The large pane-glass window framed a display of artfully arranged fabrics, all attractively draped to entice the buyer inside. Interestingly, these were not the heavy velvets and wools one might expect to see in late December, but a pastel-hued variety of light muslins better suited to Easter than Christmas. Pickett supposed the Quality (who, if the sign were to be believed, comprised Mr. Robinson's clientele) must already be thinking of their wardrobes for the coming social Season. He wondered if Lady Fieldhurst would be having new clothes made up in preparation for putting off her blacks. He wondered if there would ever come a time when he would not be constantly reminded of the lady who was, at least so far as the law was concerned, his wife.

Shaking off the unproductive train of thought, he turned his attention to the matter at hand. Nothing about the building's exterior suggested a recent burglary: all the window panes were still intact, and although the lock would require a closer examination, the door did not at first glance appear to have been forced. Even as Pickett formed this first impression, the lad announced, "Here we are," and flung open the door, setting the bell above it jangling. Pickett glanced up at it, making a mental note that anyone entering that way would find it difficult to do so without attracting the watch. Filing this information away for future consideration, he stepped inside, glanced about the dim interior, and caught his breath.

As the shop faced north, it received no direct sunlight, and the sun at this early hour on a mid-winter morning was as yet too low in the sky to provide much illumination in any case. Thus, its interior was cast into shadows, dependent on the fireplace set into the opposite wall for lighting as well as warmth. A young woman stood before the fire, the light behind her limning her hair like a halo and turning her gown to burnished gold. A dark formless shape lay at her feet, indistinguishable in the shadows. For one split second, Pickett was reminded so forcibly of his first glimpse of Lady Fieldhurst, standing before the fire in her bedchamber in just such a way with her husband's dead body at her feet, that he felt as if he'd been punched in the stomach. He stood gawking at her for a long moment, gasping for breath, until the lad, apparently judging him too stupid to speak for himself, explained, "This here's the Bow Street Runner Mr. Robinson sent for."

The young woman stepped forward away from the fire, and any resemblance to Lady Fieldhurst vanished at once. Her hair, no longer backlit by the fire, was not blonde at all, but a light brown touched with copper, and her gown was a pale yellow hue rather than white, as her ladyship's had been. Even the "body" at her feet resolved itself into an enormous dog of dubious parentage, who indicated his displeasure with this apparently mute visitor by releasing a low, rumbling growl.

"Hush, Brutus," the young woman scolded the animal, then extended her hand to Pickett. "Thank you for coming so promptly, Mr.—?"

"Pickett," he said quickly, taking her hand. "John Pickett. And you must be Mrs. Robinson?"

"Miss," she corrected him. "But Mama has been dead these seven years, so I have been the mistress of this establishment since I was twelve." She gestured toward a door in the back wall where, presumably, the despoiled safe lay. "I thought I had coped with every sort of crisis in that time, but I confess this is quite outside my experience."

Painfully aware that he was hardly presenting an image likely to fill anyone with confidence, Pickett fumbled in the pocket of his coat for his occurrence book.

"If you'll direct me to your father, I should like to ask him a few questions."

"Papa is—gone."

She offered no explanation for the linen-draper's absence, and some instinct warned Pickett not to ask for one, at least not just yet. "Perhaps you would tell me what happened, then, and show me the safe."

She nodded. "Of course. The shop was closed yesterday, since it was Sunday as well as Christmas Day, so no one has been here since Saturday. That day had been especially busy, though, since it was the last day before Christmas."

"I suppose there was plenty of money in the safe by the time the shop closed, then," Pickett observed, jotting down this information.

"Yes. In fact, it was worse than you know. Papa is expecting a new shipment from Brundy and Son this morning, and he'd made a withdrawal from the bank on Saturday in order to have sufficient funds on hand to pay for it."

Pickett looked up from his note-taking. "I should have thought it would be simpler, and safer, to pay with a bank draft."

"And so it should," she agreed. "But Mr. Brundy—the senior, that is—is rather set in his ways, and nothing will suit him but good old-fashioned pounds, shillings, and pence."

"And all this money was in the safe at the time?"

"Yes."

"How much, would you say?"

"One hundred pounds to pay for the new shipment of cloth, in addition to everything we'd taken in that day—almost two hundred pounds in all."

Pickett almost dropped his pencil. "*Two hundred pounds?* Begging your pardon, Miss Robinson, but surely your father must have known the risk he was running by keeping such a sum on hand."

She sighed. "Oh, yes, he knew. But Brundy and Son is one of our best suppliers, and their cottons are some of our most popular offerings." She glanced toward the window where, presumably, Brundy and Son fabrics were prominently displayed. "Papa hopes that when Mr. Brundy's foster son takes over the business someday, he will be open to more modern methods, but in the meantime, we dare not lose their business over what would ordinarily be a mere quibble. Now, if you'll follow me, Mr. Pickett, I'll show you the safe."

Pickett agreed, and followed her through a narrow door at the back of the shop into a second, smaller room that was clearly not open to the public. An ancient desk had been pushed against one wall, and a squat metal safe stood beside it, showing, at least at first glance, no sign of its recent violation. Still more fabrics took up what remained of the available space, not attractively displayed as the ones in the outer room were, but rolled onto bolts and stacked on shelves covering the other three walls. A young man wearing a leather apron was busily engaged in rearranging the heavy bolts, apparently making room for the new shipment.

"Leave us for now, Andrew," Miss Robinson addressed the young man, who was clearly her father's apprentice. "You can finish that later."

It had been five years since Pickett had served as apprentice to a merchant with a marriageable daughter, but he could not help feeling a certain kinship with the aproned lad who gazed at Miss Robinson with adoring eyes even as he tugged his forelock respectfully and mumbled, "Yes, miss."

Miss Robinson waited until the door closed behind him, then turned to the safe and dropped to her knees before it. She withdrew a large key from her bodice, unlocked the door of the safe, and pulled it open, then rose to her feet and stepped back to allow Pickett to examine the interior. At the back of the safe, a few short stacks of currency had been arranged according to denomination, while closer to the front coins had been similarly sorted and stacked in columns which were then arranged in rows, although a few of these had fallen, apparently knocked over during the theft.

"There appears to be quite a bit of money still here," Pickett noted in some surprise.

"Yes. We're well aware that it might have been a great deal worse."

"But why?"

She blinked at him. "I beg your pardon?"

"Why go to the trouble of breaking into a safe, only to leave a substantial sum inside? Why not take it all?"

"Really, Mr. Pickett!" Bright spots of angry color burned in her cheeks. "You sound almost as if you wish he had!"

"I beg your pardon, Miss Robinson. I meant no such thing, of course, but sometimes it helps to imagine what the criminal must have been thinking."

"Oh. Oh yes, I see. I confess, Papa and I were too grateful to see he hadn't taken it all to wonder at the reason for it." A hint of a smile lit her blue eyes. "I suppose it's unlikely he was inspired by the holiday season —you know, 'peace on earth and goodwill toward men.' "

"If that were the case, it's a pity his fit of benevolence didn't extend to abandoning the plan altogether," Pickett said, answering her smile with one of his own before raising the question that could not be postponed any longer. "But where is your Papa? I'd like to talk to him, if I may."

She let out a sigh, abandoning whimsy for the grim

realities of burglary and the loss of almost two hundred pounds sterling. "Papa has gone in search of funds. The bank is closed today, so he must beg friends to lend him sufficient money to pay for the shipment when it arrives, which ought to be—" The shrill jangling of the bell over the door interrupted her prediction—or, rather, fulfilled it. "Dear God!" she exclaimed, her eyes wide with fright. "They're here! Mr. Pickett, you must go!"

"Go? But I haven't even got started yet!" he protested.

"Oh, dear!" Wringing her hands in agitation, she cast a wild glance about the storage room. "You're too tall for us to hide you somewhere. I suppose you must come with me. Follow my lead!"

Without waiting for an answer, she squared her shoulders and sailed through the door into the showroom with her head held high and Pickett at her heels.

"Why, Mr. Brundy, we did not expect you so early!" she exclaimed with exaggerated brightness, addressing herself to a black-haired youth standing just inside the door. Beyond him, Pickett could see a tarpaulin-covered wagon standing in the street. Three or four men stood guard over it, their breath visible as wispy puffs of white, their hands shoved in pockets or tucked into their armpits for protection against the cold.

" 'Tis nigh on eight o'clock," young Brundy pointed out in accents more commonly heard in London's East

End than in this fashionable shopping district. "Not 'ardly what I'd call early."

"No, I don't suppose you would," replied Miss Robinson in just such a haughty tone as a woman of Lady Fieldhurst's class might have used to dampen the pretensions of some upstart. "But the people who patronize this establishment are Quality, and they rarely rise from their beds before noon."

Pickett, listening to this exchange, was struck by the realization that Miss Robinson did not like young Mr. Brundy. He was not quite certain why this should be so— the lad seemed perhaps a bit cocky, but otherwise unobjectionable.

"But we must not keep you standing. Andrew, Jem, go and help Mr. Brundy's men unload the wagon. Oh, Mr. Brundy, allow me to present Mr. Pickett—my young man."

This last was uttered with a hint of defiance, as if daring someone—Mr. Brundy or himself, Pickett was not quite sure which—to dispute it. Remembering her urgent instructions for him to follow her lead, Pickett merely nodded and muttered a "how do you do."

"Mr. Pickett, this is Mr. Brundy, the younger half of Brundy and Son," Miss Robinson continued. "Mr. Brundy, I'm sorry Papa isn't here to meet the shipment. This being Boxing Day, he wasn't expecting delivery until much later in the morning. He should return with your payment at any moment, if you don't mind waiting."

Beyond the window, the workmen had untied the tarpaulin and begun to fold it back, but a gesture from Mr. Brundy brought this operation to a halt.

"I'm sure *I* don't mind, miss, but me foster father'll 'ave me 'ead on a platter if I allow the men to unload before I've payment in 'and."

Miss Robinson's cheeks reddened with indignation. "Permit me to tell you, sir, that your foster father's business methods are positively antiquated!"

"Oh, you'll 'ear no argument from me," Brundy the younger said cheerfully. "I 'ope one day to change that, but in the meantime I value me 'ide too dearly to go against the old man's wishes."

If his intention was to disarm the hostile Miss Robinson, he apparently succeeded. "I wouldn't want to get you in any sort of trouble," she conceded grudgingly.

"Oh, I doubt I'd get much more than a tongue-lashing," he assured her. "Still and all, Mr. Brundy's been good to me, so I figure the least I can do is abide by 'is wishes, leastways until I can persuade 'im to give mine a try."

Upon sensing Miss Robinson's thinly veiled hostility toward the weaver's foster son, Pickett's loyalties had ranged themselves firmly with his hostess; now, however, he found himself wavering. He too felt an unpaid debt to a man who had, without the obligation of a blood tie, taken an interest in him.

"If you don't mind waiting, Mr. Brundy," Miss Robinson said, "I can offer you and your men something hot to drink and a place near the fire until Papa returns."

Young Brundy agreed to this plan, and Miss Robinson turned to her father's apprentice. "Andrew, if you will mind the shop, I will go upstairs and fetch what remains of yesterday's wassail." To Pickett, she added, "Thank you for calling, Mr. Pickett. When may I see you again?"

"Tomorrow," he said promptly. He would have preferred that afternoon, but he had no idea how long the wait might be for Mr. Robinson's return, much less how much time it would take to unload the heavily laden wagon. He would hate to put Miss Robinson in the un-comfortable position of having to arrange a second visit within the weaver's hearing, while not disclosing any hint as to its purpose.

"Tomorrow would be lovely," she assured him warm-ly. "If you will excuse me, Mr. Brundy, I'll see Mr. Pickett on his way."

She tucked her hand into the curve of his arm as she led him toward the door, addressing him in such low tones that he was obliged to bend to hear her—which, he sup-posed, added verisimilitude to her claim that he was courting her.

"Thank you for not betraying me, Mr. Pickett," she confided. "I'm sure you can understand why we don't want our suppliers to know about the theft. It wouldn't do for word to get out that Papa might be unable to pay."

"Of course," Pickett agreed, taking her hands in his and schooling his features into what he hoped was a suitably loverlike expression. "Still, it's best in such cases to make a thorough examination of the scene as soon as possible. I would be obliged if you would see that nothing is disturbed until I am able to make such an inspection tomorrow morning."

"I will do my best, and I shall warn Papa as well," she promised, giving his hands a squeeze. "Until tomorrow, then."

Chapter 5

In Which John Pickett's Investigation Takes an Unexpected Turn

The following morning, Julia arose from her bed with a lighter heart than she had felt for many a long day. She had spent the previous evening poring over the fashion plates in *La Belle Assemblée*, and had chosen four of the illustrations to take to her dressmaker: two morning gowns, a dinner dress with a short demi-train, and (her one extravagance) something suitable for evening wear: a low-necked, high-waisted gown with a sheer overskirt adorned with silk embroidery in a pattern of lilies along its hem.

Now it remained only to select the fabrics before consulting with the very expensive dressmaker who had been charged with making her wardrobe ever since she had first come to London as Frederick's bride. Impatient to put this plan into action, she made a quick breakfast of rolls and chocolate, then instructed her footman, Thomas, to send for the carriage while she made her toilette. By the time she came downstairs again, having washed, donned a carriage costume in the despised gray of half-mourning, and allowed her abigail to dress her hair, the vehicle was at the door.

"Where to, your ladyship?" called the coachman from his perch, as Thomas handed her inside.

"Number nineteen, Piccadilly," she said. "The shop of Mr. George Robinson, linen-draper."

* * *

Meanwhile, John Pickett had already set out on foot for the same location, having spent a very uncomfortable quarter-hour with his magistrate, during which he had been obliged to explain why he had elected to abandon the scene of the crime without having made even the most cursory of inspections—and making, he feared, a very poor job of defending his actions. When he reached his destination, his ears were still ringing with the vehemence of Mr. Colquhoun's unequivocally stated displeasure, and so he lost no time in examining the locks of both the safe and the shop itself in an attempt to redeem himself in his mentor's eyes. Unfortunately, these did not tell him much. Both locks were of a sort that would have been easily penetrated by any long, pointed instrument—a lady's hair-pin, for instance—by anyone who knew how; he himself could have done the thing in a matter of seconds. Still, only the most consummate of thieves would be able to accomplish the feat without leaving telltale scratches on the metal surface—and any burglar of such a caliber would be unlikely to waste his time on a linen-draper's shop when he might more profitably exercise his talents on, say, the Bank of England. But even a thorough examination with the aid of a quizzing-glass (purchased at secondhand from a pawnshop, for reasons having more to do with practicality than personal adornment) had failed to expose the slightest mark that could not be explained by over a century of daily use.

He would have reported this lack of progress to Mr. Robinson, but the proprietor was once again absent, having departed for his bank only moments before Pickett's arrival, for the purpose of withdrawing sufficient funds to repay those friends who had come to his rescue on Boxing Day.

"But if you would care to tell me," Miss Robinson assured him, "I shall be sure to pass it along to Papa."

"I'm afraid there isn't much to tell," Pickett confessed. "Whoever your unwanted visitor was, I don't see how he could have come in that door. Even if he had picked the lock—and I can't find the slightest evidence that he did— the bell over the door must have warned anyone within hearing distance that something was amiss. I suppose the shops on either side were closed as well, so late on Christmas night." Recalling his own living quarters over a chandler's shop, he gestured toward the ceiling. "Tell me, does anyone live up there?"

"Why, yes. Papa and I do."

Pickett was surprised by this revelation, having expected the prosperous shopkeeper to have made more luxurious living arrangements for himself. "And neither of you heard anything?"

She shook her head. "Not a thing."

"What about the shops next door? Are there any tenants in the upper floors?"

"The boot-maker just west of us has his workshop upstairs. I believe a clerk and his wife live in the flat over the glove shop to the east."

Pickett made a note of it in his occurrence book. "Very well, I'll have a word with them. Perhaps one of them heard some noise that might suggest an intruder."

"Begging your pardon, Mr. Pickett, but you do know, do you not, that there is a door in the back?"

Pickett, feeling more than a little foolish, admitted that no, he had *not* known. He attempted to justify himself with the recollection that he hadn't been permitted to stay long enough to find out, but suspected Mr. Colquhoun would not find this excuse any more acceptable than he did himself.

"Come here, and I'll show you."

She led him through the narrow door into the back room, then pointed toward one of the shelves stacked floor to ceiling with bolts of cloth. "Behind there," she said.

Upon closer inspection (now that he was allowed to make one, Pickett thought indignantly), the end of the shelf was not flush with the adjacent wall, as it had appeared at first glance, but offset by about three feet. A stout oak door filled the gap, looking no more promising than the front door had; in addition to a lock of the same sort that he had just inspected, this one had been fitted with a hook fastened to the door, which fitted through a corresponding eye bolted into the doorframe at about the level of Pickett's chin.

"May I?" he asked.

Upon receiving permission, he unlatched the hook and undid the lock with the key provided by Miss Robinson. He pushed the door open and leaned out. This rear door opened onto an alley, empty save for a wagon stopped some distance up the narrow street, apparently making a delivery to one of the other Piccadilly shops. Which raised another question, albeit one unrelated to the case.

"I should have thought your father would take deliveries here, instead of having workers tramping through his shop," Pickett remarked.

"And so he used to do," said Miss Robinson, her lip twist-ing scornfully, "until he allowed Mr. Brundy to persuade him that it would be good for sales if people could see when he was receiving a new shipment. Never mind the fact that traffic in Piccadilly would be tied up until the wagon was unloaded; the idea was that potential customers would be curious enough to come inside and see what new fabrics were on offer, thus stealing a march on their friends."

"Did it work?"

"It did," she conceded grudgingly.

"You don't like Mr. Brundy, do you?" Pickett observed.

She considered this statement—it wasn't exactly a question—for a long moment. "I don't *dis*like him, precisely," she said at last. "But I haven't the least desire to marry him."

"Has he asked you?" Pickett had thought the fellow looked a bit young to be thinking of marriage.

"No, but Papa has been dropping the most flagrant hints about contacting the elder Mr. Brundy and arranging a match. My only other prospect at present is Papa's apprentice, and although Papa likes Andrew well enough, he isn't at all certain he wants him to inherit the business—which my husband must eventually do, since Papa has no sons. But Papa says Mr. Brundy has a head for business, and predicts he'll do great things as soon as the elder Mr. Brundy retires and turns the reins over to him. And all of that may be true," she concluded emphatically, "but it wouldn't make up for having to hear that voice every morning over the breakfast table!"

There was nothing Pickett could say to that. His own speech had not been much better before he'd been thrown into contact with the upper classes and began, almost without conscious effort, to modulate his voice after theirs. He suspected, moreover, that one would not have to go back many generations to find the Robinson family in a very similar case—hence Miss Robinson's desire to distance herself from her own humble origins.

"But enough about me," she said, returning the subject to the business at hand. "I suppose you'll want to examine these locks as well, so I shall leave you to it. I shall be in the showroom, as will Papa after he returns, if you should need either of us."

Pickett thanked her, and after she had gone, examined the hook and eye arrangement for any sign of tampering, but found the bolts tight. He supposed the hook might possibly be lifted from the outside by means of inserting the blade of a knife between the door and its frame, but found no scratch marks on either door or frame to suggest that such an operation had been attempted. Heaving a sigh, he dropped to his knees and subjected the lock on this back door to the same inspection he'd given the one in the front—with, alas, as little to show for it. He rose to his feet and dusted off the knees of his breeches, then went to report this lack of progress to the linen-draper's daughter.

He passed through the door into the showroom, and froze in his tracks. Miss Robinson was there, just as she'd said she would be, engaged in showing a selection of filmy fabrics to a customer. And not just any customer, but a lady: a golden-haired lady clad in the lusterless gray of half-mourning.

Lady Fieldhurst, or—at least in the eyes of the law—Mrs. John Pickett.

Chapter 6

*In Which John Pickett Jumps
out of the Frying Pan and into the Fire*

Pickett ducked back through the door into the storage room and sagged against the wall, breathing hard. She was here! The lady he'd told himself he never wanted to see again was here, so close that if he were to call out to her, she would hear him. Every instinct urged him to open the door just a crack, just enough to catch one more glimpse of her, to assure himself that she was well and happy. But if she were to see him, he would be obliged to speak to her, and what could he possibly say that would not end with him begging her to drop the annulment proceedings—thus embarrassing her and humiliating himself still further? No, it was best that he remain safely out of sight until she had gone. And yet—and yet she was *there*—so close, so very close—

A low growl close at hand informed Pickett that an even nearer danger existed, and thoughts of Lady Field-hurst were temporarily set aside in favor of low-voiced assurances to Brutus that he was a good dog. Brutus, unimpressed, seemed much more concerned with ascertaining whether or not Pickett was a good man. Finding a tentative hand stretched out toward him, Brutus instantly cast his vote for the negative, and sank his teeth into the fleshy part of Pickett's hand. Choking back the howl of pain that would certainly have brought Lady Fieldhurst and everyone else in the shop running, Pickett satisfied himself with making an awkward, one-handed job of wrapping his bleeding hand in his handkerchief and tugging the knot tight with his teeth, all the while telling Brutus in an undervoice exactly what he thought of that animal's manners, morals, and parentage—a recital interrupted when the door swung open abruptly to reveal Miss Robinson, standing in the doorway exclaiming, "Why, Mr. Pickett, whatever is the matter? You look like you've just seen a ghost!"

* * *

Julia had been prepared to wait patiently in the showroom while Miss Robinson went to fetch the pale blue satin which the linen-draper's daughter was certain had been delivered only the week before, but at the sound of a familiar name, her ears pricked up. Was it possible? Could it be? A quick glance about the shop, however, revealed no glimpse of a tall young man with brown curls tied at the nape of his neck in a queue. *And what did you expect?* she chided herself silently, conscious of a vague sense of disappointment. Mr. Pickett could have no reason to patronize a linen-draper's shop, as it was unlikely that his wages, whatever they were, ran to bespoke clothing. Hard on the heels of this thought came the recollection that she knew exactly what he earned, for he had told her himself. *Unless you* want *to be a Bow Street Runner's wife and live on twenty-five shillings a week,* he'd said, hurling the words at her like a challenge—daring her to accept, knowing she could not.

Oh, really? taunted the little voice that had tormented her for the last six weeks, ever since he had first told her of their accidental marriage. *And what would you have said if he'd gone down on one knee and asked the question in earnest?*

"That is hardly the point," she muttered aloud, causing another patron to give her a curious glance.

It was nothing but the age-old lure of the forbidden, she told herself as she fixed her attention firmly on the sleek folds of satin she weighed in her hands. If he had been a gentleman of her own class, if there had been no insuperable bar to such a marriage, she would never have given him a second thought. But here, too, the little voice came back to mock her, defying her to name a single "gentleman" who would be willing to sacrifice himself for her as Mr. Pickett was . . .

"Stop it!" she hissed under her breath. "Just stop it!"

"May I help you, ma'am?" asked a young man in a leather apron, regarding her with a look of concern.

"No, thank you," Julia said, giving him a bright false smile. "The new satins are all so lovely, I'm having trouble deciding between them. Miss Robinson said something about a pale blue in the storeroom, which she's gone to find. Perhaps it will make the decision easier."

"I'm sure she'll be back with it directly," he assured her, then glanced toward the storage room door with a sullen expression. "If not, I'll go and fetch her."

No such action was necessary, for Miss Robinson came hurrying from the storeroom, breathless and rosy-cheeked and burdened with a fat bolt of shimmering blue cloth. "Here it is, your ladyship," she said, setting the new bolt down atop the others with a soft *whump*. "If you will forgive the impertinence, ma'am, the color just matches your eyes."

"So it does," Julia agreed, although in truth she had lost much of her earlier enthusiasm for the project. Still, she bought six ells of the blue satin and another three of matching net for the overskirt. The fact that she failed to notice the unseemly haste with which the linen-draper's daughter measured and cut the requested lengths said much for her own perturbation of spirits.

* * *

"I'm sorry to be so long," Miss Robinson told Pickett as she burst once more through the storage room door. "I was obliged to wait upon a customer. Now," she said briskly, dismissing Lady Fieldhurst out of hand, "let me see what that wicked dog did to you."

Thus adjured, Pickett held out his wounded hand. Miss Robinson unwrapped his makeshift bandage, all the while fussing and fretting over his injury in a manner that would have been most gratifying, had it come from a certain other female of his acquaintance.

"Come upstairs," she said at last, "and let me wash it and dress it properly for you."

Pickett consented to this plan, curious to see what the linen-draper's lodgings looked like for reasons not entirely connected to the case. This dwelling, as he saw when she opened a door halfway up the narrow, uncarpeted staircase, proved to have nothing in common with his own flat save for its location over a commercial establishment. Large windows looked down onto Piccadilly, their curtains tied back to admit the pale winter sunshine that cast checker-board patterns on the fringed carpet covering the floor and reflected off the glass protecting the framed prints on the walls.

To Pickett, whose childhood had been spent in London's worst slums, and whose cases over the past year had thrust him into the homes of some of England's wealthiest and most powerful families, the linen-draper's abode represented just the sort of respectable middle ground to which he himself might someday aspire, if he prospered in his profession. So respectable was it, in fact, that he wondered if it was quite proper for him to be here with Miss Robinson unchaperoned. Noises from the next room, however, indicated that they were not alone, and a moment later a middle-aged woman with reddened face and hands entered the room, wiping her work-roughened hands on her apron. Not Mrs. Robinson, he told himself; as he recalled, Miss Robinson had said her mother was dead. Clearly, the linen-draper's shop was profitable enough for its proprietor to afford a servant.

"Have you any hot water on the hob, Sybbie?" Miss Robinson asked without preamble. "Our wicked Brutus has bitten poor Mr. Pickett."

"Mr. Pickett, you say?" Sybbie regarded Brutus's victim speculatively, giving Pickett to understand that he was being weighed as a prospective suitor for Miss Robinson's hand.

"Mr. Pickett is from Bow Street, Sybbie. He's investigating our burglary." Miss Robinson's gently chiding tone, as well as the color that flooded her cheeks, was sufficient to inform Pickett that he had been correct in his interpretation of the older woman's motives. "Now, about that hot water—"

"Aye, miss, I'm goin', I'm goin'," she grumbled. She shuffled out of the room and returned a moment later with a bowl of water in her hands and a cloth draped over her arm.

"Thank you, Sybbie, that will be all," Miss Robinson said, when the woman seemed inclined to linger in order to observe the proceedings. Sybbie gave a little huff, but trudged away, leaving Pickett apparently alone with the linen-draper's daughter. Still, he would have bet his last week's wages that she was still within earshot—although whether the woman thought to protect Miss Robinson from any unseemly advances on his part, or merely hoped such advances might occur, he was not at all certain.

"Pray sit here, Mr. Pickett," Miss Robinson said, indicating the chair before the hearth. As he sat down, she picked up the poker and stirred the banked fire to life, then knelt at Pickett's feet, dipped the cloth into the bowl of water, and began gently swabbing his injured hand.

"I'm sure Brutus didn't mean it," she assured her patient, who was equally certain the big dog had done exactly what it had intended to do. "He's a good dog, really. He only means to protect us, poor lamb."

Of all the words Pickett might have used to describe the Robinsons' four-legged guardian, "lamb" was not one of them. Still, it would not do to cast aspersions on an animal of which Miss Robinson was obviously fond. "I won't argue the point, since you know Brutus rather better than I do," he said. "Still, I confess I feel a bit like Caesar must have done after being betrayed by *his* Brutus."

Her face lit up in a smile. "Why, Mr. Pickett! You are familiar with Shakespeare?"

"I live not far from the theatre at Drury Lane," he explained. "I go there as frequently as work and finances allow."

"Papa's business was founded in the theatre, you know," she said proudly. "My great-great—I forget how many greats—grandfather began as a costumer for the Drury Lane Theatre. He dressed the great Nell Gwyn, and when she became the, er, when she found favor with King Charles, she gave my ancestor the money to establish himself in business."

" 'Linen-draper to the Quality since 1668,' " Pickett quoted, recalling the sign over the door.

"Just so," said Miss Robinson, beaming at him.

"I suppose I must feel honored to have been bitten by a dog with such a distinguished theatrical history," Pickett said, as his nurse tore a strip of cloth and began wrapping it around his hand. "But your patrons might not feel the same, if Brutus should choose to distinguish them with the same attentions."

"Oh, but he isn't allowed in the shop where he might molest the customers," she assured him, neatly tying off her work and snipping away the excess cloth.

"I see," Pickett drawled. "That honor is reserved for me."

She dimpled at him. "Well, you *were* trespassing on his property, you know, for he considers the back room his own. Although the fault is mine," she allowed generously, "for failing to put him out into the alley behind the shop until you had finished. I hope you will forgive me."

Pickett did so readily enough, but his assurances were somewhat mechanical, as a thought had just occurred to him. "Tell me, Miss Robinson—"

"Oh, pray call me Nancy."

Pickett suddenly realized that although she had finished bandaging his hand, she still held it cradled between both of her own—and that she was gazing up at him with a warm glow in her eyes. Gently but firmly, he withdrew his hand from her grasp. "I, er, I think I'd better not," he said, and took his leave with, perhaps, more speed than grace.

* * *

So hasty was his departure, in fact, that he all but ran over a tall, cadaverous man just entering the premises as he was leaving.

"I—I beg your pardon," Pickett stammered, grabbing the man by the arms to steady him until he had regained his balance.

"My fault entirely, for not watching where I was going," the man assured him quite untruthfully. "I've had much on my mind of late, and have not been minding— and we see what has come of it."

As Pickett stooped to pick up the hat that had been knocked from his head in the mêlée, it occurred to him that here was the man he had been trying for two days to see.

"Mr. Robinson? George Robinson?" He gestured toward the sign hanging over their heads.

"Guilty as charged," the older man said, sketching a bow.

Pickett shifted his hat to his injured left hand, so that he might offer his whole right one to the linen-draper. "How do you do? I'm John Pickett, from Bow Street. I'm pleased to make your acquaintance at last, although I do regret the violence of the meeting."

"Ah, yes, Mr. Pickett. My daughter told me about you," said the linen-draper, regarding the caller with so speculative a gleam in his eye that Pickett wondered exactly what Miss Robinson had said about him. "Tell me, have you anything new to report regarding our robbery?"

"Not yet, sir, although I hope to make some progress very soon," Pickett told him. "In fact, I should like to ask you a few questions, if there is some room where we may speak uninterrupted."

"Yes, yes, of course. Come inside, and we'll go to the

back room. Nan, you and Andrew may keep an eye on things out front, there's a good girl."

"Yes, Papa." Nancy had apparently descended the stairs to the shop in Pickett's wake (albeit at a more sedate pace), and now hovered about the door. If she was disappointed at not being invited to join their conversation, she gave no outward sign, although Pickett felt her eyes following him as they passed through the showroom into the storage room at the back of the shop.

"Now, Mr. Pickett, what can I do for you?" the linen-draper asked, once they were alone in the back room with the door firmly closed behind them. Brutus emitted a low growl, and Mr. Robinson, seeing Pickett cast a wary eye in the big dog's direction, made haste to reassure him. "Pay no heed to Brutus, there. He'll not harm you."

"I hate to disagree, but as it happens, I've already made Brutus's acquaintance," Pickett said, lifting his bandaged hand.

"Have you, by gad? Well, I'm that sorry for it. I trust your injury isn't serious?"

"I don't believe it is. In any case, your daughter did a fine job of dressing it, and I am confident that the patient will live."

"Aye, she's an excellent nurse, my Nancy," boasted the linen-draper.

"I'm sure of it. Just as I am sure Brutus makes an

excellent watchdog," Pickett said, steering the conversation back to the matter at hand. "Still, I can't find that anyone heard him barking or growling on the night of the robbery."

"Aye, well, recollect that it was Christmas night," Mr. Robinson pointed out. "We'd all had a drop or two of wassail in celebration of the season, you know. I don't doubt we were all sleeping a bit more soundly than usual."

"What about bloodstains?" Pickett asked, as his gaze settled on a couple of bright red drops on the wooden floorboards where he had been standing just inside the door, safely out of sight of Lady Fieldhurst. "If Brutus felt compelled to defend the premises with his teeth, surely there must have been some evidence left behind."

"I confess I was more concerned with the condition of the safe than the state of the floorboards," the linen-draper said. "Still, if there had been any bloodstains, you can be sure my daughter would have seen them, and would have cleaned them up. A fine little housekeeper she is, my Nan."

"Er, I don't doubt it. But about the safe," Pickett said, determined not to be diverted into a discussion of Miss Robinson's domestic virtues. "I hope your losses were not too great. Is there any chance that you might be recompensed for them?"

"Insured against loss, you mean?" The linen-draper

raked long fingers through his thinning hair. "If there had been a fire, aye. I pay dues to the Sun Fire Company—you may have noticed their mark mounted on the wall, just outside the door—but only the largest commercial ventures can grease the palms of Lloyd's underwriters sufficiently to persuade them to insure against theft. It happens so frequently, you know, and the likelihood of their having to pay out is so great that the dues for that sort of protection would cost more than most thefts do. No, most of us just take what precautions we can—doors locked and bolted, a bell over the door, even a dog on the premises—and hope for the best."

"And yet all your precautions failed," Pickett noted, not without sympathy. "Tell me, Mr. Robinson, how many people have keys to the shop?"

"Three, but all of those keys are accounted for: mine, my daughter's, and Andrew's."

"Andrew's?"

"Aye, my apprentice. He comes down early every morning to light the fire, and locks up at night after me and Nancy have gone upstairs."

"He 'comes down,' you say?"

"Aye, for he has a room in the attic. So does Jem, for that matter. Jem is the lad who summoned you from Bow Street," he added, anticipating Pickett's next question.

"I see. But about Andrew—is it possible that he forgot

one of the locks that night? Someone must have heard the bell if the front door had been opened, but the one at the back—"

"No, for I checked that first thing, as soon as I saw the money was gone from the safe. Everything was locked up tight as a drum."

"Even the safe?"

"Aye, it was," the linen-draper said, much struck. "A curious thing, the thief taking the time to lock the safe back. I should have thought he would have wanted to get out as quickly as possible, wouldn't you?"

Pickett nodded. "Exactly. Whoever he was, he had no fears of being caught out before he was done." He also had no fear of Brutus, which was to Pickett's mind even more telling. Still, he didn't want to point this out, at least not yet. He didn't want to put anyone at the shop on their guard by letting them know they were themselves under suspicion.

"What about the keys to the safe?" he asked. "How many are there, and who has them?"

"There's only one, and I keep it myself."

"And yet when I inspected the safe, it was your daughter who opened it with a key she kept in her, er—" Pickett made a vague gesture in the direction of his chest.

"Aye, I left the key with her while I was gone to the bank, and told her to put it someplace where no one could get at it. No one," he repeated, and there was that in his tone, as well as his expression, that told Pickett it would have been wiser not to have mentioned where Miss Robinson had hidden the key.

"And it hasn't been out of your possession, or your daughter's, at any time?"

Mr. Robinson shook his head. "No—that is, no time lately. I did misplace it, oh, a month or so ago, but it was found within half an hour after I discovered it was missing—just before I sent for the locksmith, in fact."

"Was it indeed?" Pickett asked, his ears pricking up. "Where was it found, and by whom?"

"Jem found it lying just underneath one of the tables—the one where the new silks are displayed. Can't imagine how it got there, nor how we managed to miss it, for I would swear we searched every inch of the shop— and parts of it more than once—in that half-hour. Sometimes it seems as though objects sprout legs when no one's looking and move about on their own, doesn't it?"

"It does indeed," Pickett agreed. "Clever lad, Jem, to have found it, though. How long has he been with you?"

"About six months."

"And Andrew?" This, in fact, interested Pickett far more than the boy, Jem, did.

"He's been with me for nigh on ten years, ever since he was nobbut a lad of twelve."

A lad of twelve, Pickett thought. A twelve-year-old boy would have little interest in a girl very nearly his own age. A young man of two-and-twenty, however, thrown into daily contact with an attractive young woman of similar age was a very different matter. And who better to favor Pickett with a candid opinion of that young man than another, a still younger man who might be a rival for the same young woman's affections?

Having discovered, at least for the nonce, all he could from the linen-draper, Pickett took his leave and headed back toward Bow Street, where he planned to report back to his magistrate before setting out for the City, and the London warehouse of Brundy and Son.

Chapter 7

*In Which Messrs. Pickett and Brundy Exchange
Philosophies on Courtship, Marriage, and Other Things*

"Hullo, what's this?" demanded Mr. Colquhoun when
Pickett returned to Bow Street with one hand swathed in
bandages.

"Oh, that," Pickett said, glancing dismissively at his
injured hand. "Just a small disagreement with an over-
protective watchdog. The dog won," he added un-
necessarily.

"Shall I send for a physician?" the magistrate asked in
some concern, lifting his hand to summon a messenger.

"No, no, that won't be necessary," Pickett assured him
hastily. "It's hardly more than a scratch, really, and Miss
Robinson washed and dressed it."

Mr. Colquhoun's bushy eyebrows rose. "Miss Robinson, you say?"

Pickett nodded. "The linen-draper's daughter."

"I see." The magistrate regarded him with a speculative gleam in his eye. "Is she pretty?"

"I fail to see what that has to do with anything," Pickett said, very much on his dignity.

"Then I fear you haven't half the intelligence I'd credited you with," the magistrate informed him bluntly. "In all seriousness, John, females do tend to form sentimental attachments to the men they nurse. You might do far worse than a merchant's daughter."

It was true, Pickett knew, and yet there was more than one barrier to such a match. "I know you're right, sir, and I will admit that yes, Miss Robinson is very pretty. But setting aside the fact that I already have a wife—" Mr. Colquhoun dismissed this circumstance with a snort of derision. "—I'm sure you would advise me to be certain Miss Robinson hasn't been helping herself to the contents of her father's safe before making any overtures in that direction."

"Very true," conceded his mentor. "Have you any reason to believe she has been?"

"N-no," Pickett said slowly, considering the matter. "But I think it very likely that someone in the shop has. There were no scratches or any other markings to indicate that the lock had been forced, and no one recalls hearing the bell ring, or the dog bark."

"That would be the same dog that, er—?" Mr. Colquhoun's inquiring gaze dropped to Pickett's bandaged hand.

"The very same, sir."

"Yes, unless for some reason this dog finds your presence uniquely repugnant, I agree that it sounds as if the intruder must have been someone familiar to him," the magistrate concurred. "So, what is to be your next move? Have you decided?"

Pickett let out a sigh, and leaned against the wooden railing that fronted the magistrate's bench. "I should like to find out what I can about the characters of some of the persons involved. The younger Mr. Brundy of Brundy and Son might be a likely source of information. He delivers cottons to Mr. Robinson's shop, and his foster father, the senior partner, insists on payment upon delivery and in cash. Miss Robinson seems to think the old man is merely being disagreeable, but it occurs to me that he might have other reasons for refusing to extend credit to her father."

Mr. Colquhoun nodded in agreement. "Very well, Mr. Pickett, I believe you can find the Brundy warehouse in Cheapside. Near Queen Street, if memory serves."

"Thank you, sir," Pickett said, and turned to go.

"Oh, and John," the magistrate's voice called him back.

"Yes, sir?"

"Be careful of any dogs that may cross your path, will you?"

Pickett acknowledged this verbal hit with a rueful grin

and a wave of his bandaged hand, then set out on foot for the City.

* * *

Upon reaching the warehouse of Brundy and Son, Pickett stepped inside and blinked in amazement. As his eyes adjusted to the dim light, he found himself standing in a cavernous room filled with row upon row of shelves, each one stacked floor to ceiling with bolts of fabric in every color of the rainbow, and of every pattern from demure floral prints to bold Greek key designs. He collared the first person he saw and, in a voice echoing weirdly in the vast space, requested a word with Mr. Brundy.

"I hope you've got a good set of lungs, then," came the reply. "They'll have to be, for him to hear you all the way in Lancashire."

"He isn't in London, then?" Pickett asked, deflated.

"Didn't I just say so? He lets young Ethan come to Town twice a year to handle all the London business. If you want one of the Brundys, you'll have to make do with him."

Pickett castigated himself for not making it clear at the outset precisely which Brundy he wished to interview. Privately, he considered Ethan Brundy rather young to be trusted with the London side of what was apparently a very large business concern but, remembering how frustrated (and, yes, insulted) he'd often felt by disparaging references to his own age, he resolved to give the fellow the benefit of the doubt. "Very well, where can I find him?"

"He'll be in his office."

The man jerked his thumb toward the back of the warehouse, but made no offer to accompany him. Pickett thanked him for the information, and set out in the direction he had indicated. Thankfully, he met Mr. Brundy halfway, coming toward the front of the building as Pickett headed toward the rear. Each sighted the other at exactly the same time, and both stopped in mutual recognition.

"Mr.—Pickett, is it?" Brundy asked in the same unrefined accents Pickett had noted the day before. "Nancy Robinson's intended?"

"Yes and no," Pickett said, grimacing at the thought that by claiming him as her "young man," Miss Robinson might have prejudiced young Brundy against him. "I should like a word with you, if you can spare a minute."

"Aye, if you'll follow me," he agreed, eyes bright with curiosity as he led the way to the small office carved out of one corner at the back of the warehouse. He closed the door, shutting out the din on the other side, then seated himself behind the desk, leaned back in his chair and propped his booted feet on its scarred surface. "Now," he said, his voice strangely loud now that it no longer echoed, "what do you want from me?"

"I should like you to tell me what you know about George Robinson."

"Wanting inside information on your future papa-in-law, are you?" Ethan Brundy grinned knowingly, and something about his smile was so engaging that Pickett wanted to smile back in spite of the fact that the fellow had entirely the wrong idea about him and Miss Robinson.

Pickett shook his head. "No, I'm not. That is, I do want inside information on Mr. Robinson, if you have any to give me, but not on his daughter's account. In fact, I'd never laid eyes on Miss Robinson until yesterday."

Young Brundy let out an appreciative whistle. "Fast worker, aren't you?"

"Look here," Pickett said impatiently, "I'm not really courting Miss Robinson. She only said that because she doesn't want to be pressured into marriage with you. I'm sorry if you had hopes in that direction, but there it is."

Brundy sat up abruptly with his feet on the floor, staring at Pickett in astonishment. "And 'oo said I wanted to marry 'er?"

"Well, no one, exactly," Pickett admitted. "But apparently Mr. Robinson has some idea of broaching the subject with your foster father—a sort of business merger, as I understand it, as well as a personal one."

" 'e'll catch cold at that, 'e will," Brundy predicted

confidently. "Mr. Brundy is quite 'appy with 'is business just the way it is. As for me and Nancy, well, I'm sure she's a very nice girl, but I 'aven't the least desire to marry 'er."

He spoke so emphatically that Pickett drew the logical conclusion. "I take it your affections are engaged elsewhere?"

"No," Brundy confessed cheerfully. "In fact, I 'aven't yet met the woman I'd like to marry, but I'm in no 'urry. I figure I'll know 'er when I see 'er."

"If only it were that easy," Pickett muttered.

"What do you mean?" asked the weaver, much struck. Clearly, any such complication had never occurred to him.

"Only that the lady might have other ideas," Pickett pointed out with some asperity, nettled by the younger man's easy confidence.

"In that case, I'll 'ave a bit of work to do, won't I?" young Brundy said, undaunted.

There was nothing Pickett could say to this. He'd *known* (as Mr. Brundy had put it) from the moment he'd seen Lady Fieldhurst standing over her husband's dead body—but he also knew that he could work his fingers to the bone, and it still wouldn't make him an eligible match for her. He hardly knew whether to wish Brundy luck in his courtship of the theoretical female of his choice, or to hope she led him a merry dance, if for no other reason than to shake the fellow's extraordinary self-assurance.

"That's as may be," he said, "but I didn't come to discuss your marriage prospects—or mine, for that matter. I came to learn what I could about George Robinson."

"Right you are, then. What do you want to know?"

"What sort of man would you say he is? Is he honest?"

Mr. Brundy seemed to have no doubts on this head. "Me foster father wouldn't do business with 'im if 'e wasn't."

"And yet he—your foster father, that is—insists on being paid up front, and in cash," Pickett pointed out.

"Aye, but 'e's that way with everyone. 'E's a shrewd 'ead for business, 'as old Mr. Brundy, but tough as an old boot, 'e is. Some of 'is ideas are a bit old-fashioned, but 'e won't 'ear of changing them."

"So this isn't a business practice reserved for George Robinson?"

"Lord, no! I can't tell you the brangles we've 'ad over it—that, and other business practices, for that matter."

"I see," said Pickett, mentally crossing George Robinson off his list.

"Say, if you don't mind me asking, what's your interest in George Robinson? Setting aside 'is daughter, of course."

Pickett struggled with his conscience. If Miss Robinson were to be believed, her father was going to considerable lengths to make sure no one knew about the recent robbery. And yet, it was impossible to solve a crime while keeping secret the fact that one had been committed. The shopkeepers on either side, for instance, had answered Pickett's questions readily enough, but had almost certainly drawn their own conclusions as to why he was asking them. And why shouldn't they? If there was a robber at large, he couldn't blame them for wanting to know, so they might take whatever precautions they could.

"There was a robbery at Mr. Robinson's shop on Christmas night," he said at last, laying all his cards on the table, "and I was summoned to investigate. I'm with Bow Street," he added by way of explanation.

"Are you, by Jove?" exclaimed Brundy. "I'd always thought you fellows were older."

Pickett was accustomed (though by no means resigned) to hear disparaging remarks about his age, but he would be hanged if he would allow such comments from a fellow several years younger than himself. "Look, let's reach an agreement before we go any further, shall we? You don't make any unwanted observations about my age, and I won't make any about yours."

"Fair enough," said the weaver, with a rueful grin that gave Pickett to understand he was not the only one plagued by such remarks.

"As I was saying, about this robbery—there's no evidence of forced entry, but a considerable amount of money was taken from the safe. Between you and me and the lamppost, it appears to be the work of someone inside."

"There you are, then," declared Ethan Brundy, spreading his hands. "If I were a betting man, I'd put me money on that fellow Andrew."

Pickett had reached the same supposition, but he was well aware that his magistrate was not an admirer of unsubstantiated hunches. "Do you mind telling me how you came to that conclusion?"

"Plain as a pikestaff, innit? 'e's 'ead over 'eels for Nancy, but 'asn't a chance of marrying 'er unless 'e comes into money from somewhere. 'Tis only natural 'e'd be tempted."

Pickett took instant exception to this assumption. "I beg to differ! I was once apprenticed to a coal merchant, and it never crossed my mind to steal from him in order to marry his daughter!"

"Aye, well, we can't all be the paragons you Bow Street men are," Brundy said by way of apology. "I grew up rough, you know—in the work'ouse 'til I was nine."

"Tell me about rough," Pickett retorted, bristling. "I grew up picking pockets in Covent Garden."

"I never knew 'oo me father was," recalled Mr.

Brundy, with a soulful look in his brown eyes.

"I knew who mine was, for it was he who taught me how to pick pockets. And a good thing, too, or else I'd have starved after he was transported to Botany Bay."

"All right, then," Brundy pronounced, "you win."

"Win what?" asked Pickett, all at sea.

The ' 'ard cheese' competition," the weaver explained, as if it should have been obvious.

Until that moment, Pickett had not realized he was jealous of the younger man's rosier prospects. Nor, now that he had been made aware of it, was he proud of the fact. He gave a sheepish little laugh. "I beg your pardon. I had not meant—"

"Never mind that," Brundy said, dismissing Pickett's apology with a wave of his hand. "I'll admit, though, to being curious as to what your da thinks of you working for Bow Street. Seems to me 'e might consider that you've gone over to the enemy."

Pickett nodded emphatically. Now that the uncomfortable moment of self-realization was past, he found he could confide things in Brundy that no one else, not even his sympathetic magistrate, could begin to understand. "He would, which is why I've never told him. I send him half of my wages every month, though, and if he wonders where I'm earning it, he's never written to ask."

"If 'e knew, would 'e still take it?"

Pickett gave a snort of derision. "My da, turn down more than two quid a month? Surely you jest!"

In spite of his humble origins, Ethan Brundy possessed a mind as quick as Pickett's own, and from this bitter statement deduced a very fair estimate of Pickett's earnings—accurate enough, in any case, to know that they were scarcely sufficient to support two separate households in anything approaching comfort. "But you fellows are sometimes given rewards for solving cases, aren't you, over and above your regular wages?"

"We are, but I—I don't usually share them with Da." It was his guilty secret, this hoarding of the rewards that occasionally came his way. He told himself it was because his father would demand the details of exactly how he'd come by ten or even twenty pounds all at once—assuming, of course, that these riches survived the six-month voyage without being stolen by the ship's passengers, many of whom were transported criminals themselves. If he were honest, though, he carefully squirreled away these larger sums, as if he might someday accumulate enough to make him an acceptable husband for Lady Fieldhurst. Brushing aside this forlorn hope, he said aloud, "In any case, Mr. Robinson has offered no such incentive, and it's unlikely that he would be inspired to reward me for depriving him of an apprentice."

"Per'aps not, but 'e might feel grateful to you for

saving 'is daughter from marrying that same apprentice, especially if 'e turned out to be a criminal," Brundy observed. " 'Tis a pity you can't plant enough money in the safe to tempt the robber—'ooever 'e might be—to 'ave another go at it."

"Y-yes," Pickett said slowly, drumming his fingers thoughtfully on the desk. "Yes, it is."

Chapter 8

In Which John Pickett Proposes a Scheme

"You want to *what?*" demanded Mr. Colquhoun, when his most junior Runner arrived in Bow Street breathless with exertion, having run most of the way from the City.

"I want to break into Mr. Robinson's shop," Pickett repeated eagerly. He took advantage of his magistrate's momentary speechlessness to explain. "If we can somehow contrive to make sure the safe contains a large sum of money—or at least make certain persons *think* it contains a large sum of money—perhaps our robber would be willing to try again. But I would break into the back room myself sometime after the family had gone to bed, and I would be lying in wait for him. I could catch him in the act."

"I don't doubt your sincerity, John, but—" Mr. Colquhoun broke off, words apparently failing him.

Pickett's face fell. "I wouldn't take anything, sir, if that's what worries you. I won't even open the safe, only the back door. I made you a promise ten years ago, and I've kept it."

"It isn't that—" the magistrate began. And nor was it—at least, not exactly. He had every confidence in John Pickett's integrity. And yet . . . who could say how a man, *any* man, might respond when confronted with sufficient temptation? Let alone a very young man with a criminal background who dared to love a lady who was, at least in the eyes of Society, as far above him as the stars above the heavens—and whose affections had remained constant in the face of demands that would have made many an older and wiser man turn tail and run. No, to a man capable of such steadfastness, the keeping of a ten-year-old promise should be no very great challenge. It was not John Pickett's morals, but his own judgment he doubted. If he were to discover after all these years that his trust in and, yes, affection for the lad had been misplaced, he was not at all sure he could bear it. He was quite certain that John Pickett would fail to recognize the distinction, however—which was probably just as well, since he could not have explained it in a way that made any sense, even to himself.

On the other hand, he had not seen his protégé so animated in many weeks—since before the annulment business, in fact.

"Oh, very well," he conceded grudgingly, and was rewarded with a radiant smile from the young man—a smile all the more dazzling for being so rarely seen.

"Thank you, sir! You won't regret it, I—"

"You just be careful, and mind you're not taken up by the watch," growled the magistrate, cutting off Pickett's protestations of thanks. "A pretty fool I'll look, if one of Bow Street's principal officers is arrested for breaking and entering."

"I will—that is, I won't be, sir, I promise."

"And the dog?" Mr. Colquhoun gestured toward Pickett's bandaged hand.

"I've thought of that, sir, and I think I know a way around it."

"Hmmp," was the noncommittal reply. "Now, if you intend to be capering about at all hours of the night, you'd better take yourself off and try to catch forty winks while you can."

"Yes, sir." Pickett agreed readily enough, but showed no sign of leaving.

"Well, what is it?"

"Er, there remains the question of how to bait the trap with enough money to tempt a thief, sir."

"You just leave that to me. Now, be off with you."

"Yes, sir," said Pickett, and reluctantly took his leave, recognizing that his magistrate had no intention of confiding in him just how this feat was to be accomplished.

"Reckless young cub," Mr. Colquhoun grumbled,

watching him go. Raising his voice, he called, "Mr. Maxwell! I'm going home to share a quick nuncheon with my wife. I should be back within the hour, but until I return, you're in charge."

This practice was so unusual that Janet Colquhoun was hardly more surprised than Mr. Maxwell had been.

"Why, what a pleasant surprise," she said, lifting her face to be kissed. "What brings you home so early?"

"Is it so unusual for me to want to partake of a crust of bread before my own hearth, in the bosom of my own family?" he responded, bending to give her a peck on the cheek.

"Well, yes," came the candid reply.

Ignoring this assertion, he bent a critical gaze upon her soft cashmere morning gown with its fashionable high waist and frill of white lawn at the neck. "Janet, my dear," he said, "how long has it been since you had a new dress?"

* * *

In the meantime, Pickett did not go straight home, but stopped first at a butcher's shop and bought three somewhat scrawny lamb chops. When he reached Drury Lane, he presented these to Mrs. Catchpole, his landlady and the proprietor of the chandler's shop over which he resided, cutting off her exclamations over his bandaged hand.

"It's fine, really it is," he assured her. "But look what I've brought. If you'll cook two of these for my dinner, you can have the third for yourself," he offered.

She regarded him warily, but curiosity soon won out. She took the package, untied the string, and spread the newspaper wrappings. "Bless my soul!" she exclaimed delightedly. "Aye, I'll cook them for you, Johnny, and a nice potato to go with them besides. We'll dine like the Lord Mayor himself tonight, just see if we don't!"

Privately, Pickett rather doubted this, but thanked her nonetheless (thinking rather guiltily that he should have made such a gesture before, and without ulterior motives, seeing it meant so much to her), then climbed the stairs to his own flat. Here he pulled the curtains tight to shut out the light, then shed his coat, waistcoat, and cravat before sitting on the edge of the bed and taking off his shoes. He unbuttoned the collar of his shirt, then stretched out full length on the narrow bed and pulled the oft-darned blanket up to his chin, all set to snatch what sleep he could in preparation for the night's clandestine activities.

He awoke some time later to find the room in shadows and, when he pulled back the curtain, found that dusk had fallen. He had no time to lose, if he was to visit Mr. Robinson's shop before that establishment closed for the night. Shoving his feet into his shoes, he snatched up cravat and knotted it hastily about his neck, then hastily donned his coat and waistcoat before heading back out, locking the door to his flat behind him.

"Going out again?" exclaimed Mrs. Catchpole in some dismay, hearing his footsteps on the stairs.

"Only for a little while," he assured her. "I'll be back in plenty of time for those lamb chops, believe me! Although," he added, seeing a potential pitfall, "I will have to go out again, quite late, and I don't know when I'll be back. I'll try to be quiet so as not to wake you up, but please don't be alarmed if you should hear me."

She made the usual halfhearted complaint about how he needed a wife (predicting confidently that any woman worth her salt would soon put an end to his rackety ways), and offered once again, without much hope, to introduce him to her niece Alice, but let him go with no further protest.

He arrived at George Robinson's shop in Piccadilly to find the shop's inventory much depleted. The counter was littered with wooden spools that had once held ribbons or lace, and several of the tables (including the one he had seen freshly stocked with muslins from Brundy and Son only the day before) were practically empty. As for the linen-draper and his daughter, they—indeed, the entire staff—appeared to be in a state of imperfectly concealed excitement, although whether their underlying emotion was pleasure or distress, he could not tell. The answer, as it turned out, was both.

"The biggest single order we've ever had," Nancy

Robinson confided eagerly. "Over a hundred pounds, all told."

"W-what—? Who—?" Pickett stammered.

Fortunately, Miss Robinson had no difficulty understanding the questions that Pickett could not quite wrap his tongue around. "A fine Scottish lady and her three grown daughters, all buying fabrics for new clothes for themselves and their children."

"Scottish, you say?" echoed an enthralled John Pickett, recalling the large and noisy Colquhoun family.

"Aye, and so funny their accents were! And they paid in cash, mind you, so I think they must be very rich, don't you?"

"Undoubtedly," agreed Pickett, struggling to hide a smile at his magistrate's ingenuity. *Leave it to me*, indeed!

"Only it was too late to take it to the bank, so all that money must stay in the safe until tomorrow morning— which has us all a little nervous, after what happened last time."

"Yes, I can see how it might," Pickett said.

"Do you think we should post a guard overnight?" she asked, struck by sudden inspiration.

"*No!* That is, no, Miss Robinson, I don't think that will be necessary," he amended, a bit more moderately. "I would gladly stay and stand guard myself, but I already have plans for the evening," he said with perfect truth.

"Still, I can't imagine anyone would take such a risk a second time, not so soon after the first."

"I suppose you're right," she said doubtfully. "But I confess I should sleep easier if you were to look things over while you're here."

As this dovetailed perfectly with his own plans, he readily agreed. He allowed her to lead him through the door into the back room, where he tested the locks of both safe and back door, all the while calculating what tools might be most effective for breaching them. At last, having satisfied both his own ends and those of Miss Robinson, he took his leave and returned to his own lodgings to make preparations.

Chapter 9

In Which John Pickett Reverts
to His Old Way of Life

Back at his two-room flat in Drury Lane, Pickett made his preparations with the solemnity of one preparing for a sacred rite. He checked the coal-scuttle on the hearth and, finding the bottom of it covered with a thick layer of black dust, removed the bowl and pitcher from the washstand and set the coal-scuttle in its place. He next turned his attention to the bureau drawers where his meager wardrobe was stored, selecting the oldest (and therefore the dingiest) shirt he owned and laying it out on the bed. A pair of black breeches came next, followed by black stockings and a black cravat. He suffered a small pang upon removing his black tailcoat from its peg on the wall. It was the best he owned, and usually reserved for court appearances at the Old Bailey; he could only hope that it would suffer no irreversible ill-effects from the indignities he was about to inflict upon it. If his hopes were doomed to disappointment, however, perhaps Mrs. Catchpole might be persuaded (for something in addition to the modest sum he paid her above and beyond his monthly rent in exchange for laundering his clothing) to work some magic with damp tea leaves and fuller's earth. In any case, he had no choice. The black tailcoat joined the other garments on the bed.

His preparations were interrupted at this point by a tapping on the door of the outer room. He left the bedroom, pulling the door closed behind him, and opened the outer door to find Mrs. Catchpole standing there holding a tray covered with a checked cloth. He didn't have to lift the cloth to see what was underneath; the aroma of lamb chops was sufficient to inform him that this was his supper. He thanked her profusely, but carefully avoided saying anything that she might interpret as an invitation to linger.

After she had gone, he set the tray on the table and removed the cloth. Two lamb chops, still sizzling, held pride of place on a blue-rimmed stoneware plate, accompanied by a potato, a hunk of bread, and a small crock of butter. With a whimper of regret, Pickett removed the two chops and wrapped them carefully in a napkin. Desire warred with necessity for a long moment before Pickett yielded to the former. He unfolded the napkin and took one bite out of the larger of the two chops, then wrapped them back up and made what supper he could from the potato, bread, and butter.

And then there was little he could do but wait. He drew up a chair before the fire and selected a book from the modest collection of secondhand volumes arranged on the mantel, then read by the light of the fire while he listened for the periodic chiming of the church bells of St. Mary-le-Strand. Finally, as the bells signaled eleven, he laid aside his book and returned to the bedroom, where he arrayed himself in the funereal garments he'd laid out earlier, taking care to spread out the folds of the cravat in order to cover as much of his pale shirtfront as he could contrive.

His costume complete, he turned his attention to assembling the necessary tools. He returned to the sitting room for the knife with which he'd buttered his bread, carefully wiped it clean, then put it in the inside breast pocket of his coat. On second thought, he reflected, the streets of London could be dangerous so late at night. He removed the knife from his pocket and slid it up his shirtsleeve with its handle down and held loosely in place by the wristband. Granted, it was too blunt to be of much use as a weapon, but if self-defense should suddenly become necessary, it would be better than nothing.

Next, he rummaged in the top drawer of his bureau until he located a hairpin. It was an odd thing, perhaps, to find in a bachelor's lodging, but then, this was no ordinary hairpin. It had once belonged to *her*, had been plucked from her hair by her own fingers for a very similar purpose as the one it would serve tonight. He smiled a little, remembering that earlier occasion, for it had also been the first time he had kissed her. Actually, if he were to be honest, it had been she who had kissed him, and although he reminded himself that there had been nothing at all romantic about the encounter—after all, they'd had to have *some* reason for being alone together in a supposedly locked room in the middle of the night—he could never quite make himself believe it. He should have returned it to her, of course; he'd meant to, but the dual traumas of being simultaneously discovered and kissed had driven the matter from his mind. He hadn't realized it was still in his possession until after he'd returned to London and turned out his pockets, and although he had longed for some excuse to see her again, even he had recognized the return of a hairpin as the flimsiest of excuses. And so he had kept it like a talisman, and tonight it would be almost like having her there beside him. Or so he told himself, as he slipped it into the inside breast pocket of his coat.

There was only one thing left to do. No, two. He fetched the packet of lamb chops from the table in the sitting room and tucked them into his pocket along with the hairpin; he only hoped he would not have every stray dog and cat in London following in his wake by the time he reached Piccadilly. Finally, he plunged his hands into the coal dust at the bottom of the scuttle and liberally smeared his face with black. In addition to making him less visible inside the darkened shop, this last would also provide him with a disguise along the way, should one be necessary; he had only to take a few staggering steps and sing a few off-key bars of "Drink to Me Only With Thine Eyes" to be taken for any coal worker, or perhaps a chimney sweep, out drinking his wages.

At last, the bells of St. Mary-le-Strand chimed the half-hour, and he picked up his shoes (he'd warned Mrs. Catchpole he would be going out, but he had no desire to tempt fate) and tiptoed down the staircase in his stockinged feet. At the foot of the stairs, he put on his shoes, and a moment later he was weaving his way down Drury Lane toward the Strand and thence to Pall Mall—and only the keenest of observers might have noticed that his steps, unsteady as they were, bore unvaryingly southwestward. Determined to display nothing stealthy in his manner, he soon was emboldened to interrupt his song long enough to call a cheery (if slurred) "Ev'nin'!" to the few persons out and about at such an hour.

Unfortunately, he had reckoned without the nocturnal habits of the upper class. As he approached the place where Piccadilly connected with Jermyn Street via St. James's, he recognized an acquaintance (he could hardly call him a friend), no doubt returning to his Albany flat from one of the Jermyn Street gaming hells. The sight was so unexpected, and so unwelcome, that had he actually been drunk he would certainly have been shocked into sobriety.

"*Mr. Pickett?*" exclaimed Lord Rupert Latham, in accents as stunned as Pickett's would have been, had he been capable of speech. Unlike Pickett, however, his lordship quickly recovered his poise. "I trust you will forgive me for asking, but have you perchance fallen into a coal-cellar?"

Giving himself a moment to gather his wits, Pickett leaned forward to examine the speaker closely through narrowed eyes, careful to hold his breath (which would, of course, betray no trace of strong drink). "I know who you are," he pronounced at last, drawing himself up to his full height. "You're L-Lord R-Rupert."

"Very perceptive of you," his lordship acknowledged, "especially given your present condition. Dare I assume that this overindulgence—which I will pay you the compliment of saying seems strangely unlike you—means your 'marriage' has been voided?"

"M-my marriage?" Pickett echoed stupidly.

"To the Lady Fieldhurst," Lord Rupert explained obligingly.

"Not L-Lady Fieldhurst," Pickett corrected him. "Mrs. Pickett." He uttered this last with painstakingly correct pronunciation.

"As you wish. Although not for much longer, one trusts."

"I'll th-thank you not to b-bandy m'wife's name about in th'street," Pickett said with as much dignity as a supposedly drunken man might be able to muster.

"Very true. How lowering it is to have my manners corrected by, er, an inebriated Bow Street Runner! Now, if you will pardon me for cutting this charming encounter short, I must away to my humble abode. I suddenly find myself possessed of a burning desire to pay a morning call tomorrow on a certain lady of our acquaintance, and for this I require a good night's repose. Adieu, Mr. Pickett! Your most obedient servant."

Lord Rupert swept a bow that was insulting in its very obeisance—which Pickett returned with gratitude, as it allowed him to conceal any pain his face might have betrayed at the realization that he was not to be allowed to keep even so much as his lady's good opinion. As he and Lord Rupert parted company, he forced himself to pick up the threads of his song.

"Or leave a kiiiiss but in the cuuuup, And IIII'll not ask for wiiiine . . ."

He reached the shop of George Robinson without further incident, and looked up at the windows of its upper floors in order to satisfy himself that everyone was abed.

Finding all the windows dark, he retraced his steps up Piccadilly and approached the shop once more, this time by way of the alley running along the back. He fumbled in his coat pocket for the hairpin, then knelt before the door, reflecting that, after his encounter with Lord Rupert, picking a lock would be mere child's play. He inserted the hairpin into the lock, pressed his ear to the door, and manipulated the pin in the lock until he heard a faint *click.* Testing the knob, he found that it now turned easily in his hand. Having dealt efficiently with the lock, he stood up, drew the knife from his sleeve, and turned his attention to the hook that had been fastened at, if memory served, about the level of his chin. He inserted the blade of the knife between doorframe and panel, then moved it first up and then down, until it met with resistance. Yes, there it was. He withdrew the knife and inserted it again beneath the obstruction, then slid the blade upward until he could feel the resistance yield as the hook disengaged from its eye. Still holding it up with the blade of the knife, he grasped the knob and eased the door open.

And was met by Brutus, baring his teeth and growling ominously.

This time, however, Pickett was prepared. "No, I haven't forgotten you," he assured the dog, his voice scarcely more than a whisper. "See, I've brought you something."

He withdrew the packet of chops from his pocket, unwrapped the napkin, and tossed the contents across the room. Brutus, nothing loth, gave chase at once, scampering across the room like a puppy in pursuit of his prize. With the dog's attention otherwise engaged, there was nothing to prevent Pickett from entering the back room and closing the door softly behind him, re-engaging the locks so that no intruder might have advance warning of anything amiss. Having taken this precaution, he settled himself in a corner of the room that offered an unobstructed view of the safe while leaving him in shadows, virtually invisible except for the whites of his eyes, should anyone enter the room carrying a light.

As he sat in the stygian darkness with no way to amuse himself and nothing to occupy his mind, it seemed to Pickett as if the moments crawled by, or even stopped altogether. He leaned his head against the wall and closed his eyes. He would look a pretty fool in the morning, if he were to be discovered here in the morning with nothing to show for his vigil. Mr. Colquhoun might not be too pleased either, come to that, although his wife would certainly have no cause for complaint . . .

He had begun to drift off to sleep when a small sound jerked him instantly awake. A moment later the door to the showroom opened, and a solitary figure entered the room, an anonymous silhouette bearing a single candle in its hand. Pickett held his peace, watching silently as the figure set the candle on the floor beside the safe and knelt before it. Pickett could not have seen what happened next even had there been sufficient light, for his view was blocked by the figure itself. Still, he was sufficiently well-versed in safecracking to recognize the sound of a lock being released, and the creak of the hinges as the door swung open.

The candle was taken up again, no doubt to better illuminate the interior of the safe, and although Pickett could not see what transpired, he was certain enough that when the safe door creaked shut and the dark figure took up its candle once more, he judged it time to make his presence known. Before the thief could make his exit, Pickett spoke out of the darkness.

"How now, Andrew?"

Chapter 10

In Which John Pickett Catches a Thief

The candle was immediately snuffed, and the sharp smell of smoke filled the room. In the next instant the door into the showroom was flung open, and Pickett leaped to his feet and gave chase as his quarry beat a hasty retreat. Alas, his opponent had a distinct advantage, possessing long familiarity with the layout of the shop, and Pickett banged his hip painfully against a corner of the counter as he pursued the thief, who appeared to be making for the stairs. Thankfully, Pickett discovered an unexpected ally in Brutus, who, finding his new friend and his old one engaged in some sort of game (and one, moreover, that he with his keen canine eyesight should easily win), threw himself into the general confusion, giving voice to his pleasure in the sport with barks of delight.

Some time later (it seemed to Pickett like hours, although it could not have been more than a minute or two), a clatter of footsteps sounded on the stairs, and a moment later Mr. Robinson and his daughter burst into the room, both in their nightclothes and the latter with her light brown hair in a single braid down her back. They each held a candle, and the feeble light of these two flames was sufficient to illuminate two men grappling about on the floor.

"Andrew!" cried Miss Robinson, recognizing only one of the two. "What are you doing?"

"Stop this brawling and get up, both of you," commanded the linen-draper with an air of dignity quite out of keeping with his *déshabillé*.

The two obliged, albeit slowly and stiffly, and Miss Robinson gasped as the identity of the second of the combatants became clear.

"Now," continued Mr. Robinson, "perhaps you'll tell me what this is all about."

"Very well," Pickett began, but the apprentice interrupted.

"I heard a noise, and came down to find this fellow breaking into the shop. Small wonder he didn't want a guard posted!"

Two pairs of eyes shifted from one man to the other, weighing the word of a Bow Street Runner of three days' acquaintance against that of a young man they had known since he was a boy.

"Mr. Pickett?" Nancy Robinson addressed him

uncertainly, and Pickett became uncomfortably aware of his incriminating costume and blackened face.

"It's true that I broke into the shop," Pickett confessed, "but only for the purest of motives. I knew there was a large sum of money in the safe, and thought there was a good chance that whoever had stolen from you the first time might think a second attempt worth the risk. So I broke in and waited in the dark for him—and as you see, I was right."

"Are you saying that Andrew—*Andrew,* who has been with me for these last ten years—has been stealing from me?" demanded the linen-draper.

"He's lying!" put in the apprentice.

"I know how this must pain you, sir, and I'm sorry for it," said Pickett, ignoring the outburst, "but yes. If you doubt it, you have only to ask us both to turn out our pockets."

He did not wait for the order, but reached into the inside breast pocket of his coat and began removing the tools of his erstwhile trade and laying them out on the counter: a knife with a thin blade, a lady's hairpin, and a handkerchief smelling strongly of lamb chops.

"I thought it best to cultivate a friendship with Brutus," Pickett said by way of explanation for this last, then folded the grease spots to the inside and wiped the worst of the coal dust from his face.

"Forgive me, Mr. Pickett, if the contents of your pockets don't exactly fill me with confidence!" snapped Mr. Robinson.

"No, sir, nor would I expect them to—at least, not until you compare them to Andrew's."

The linen-draper nodded. "Fair enough, Mr. Pickett. Well, Andrew, let's have it, then."

Finding all eyes watching him expectantly, Andrew hesitated for only a moment, then turned and bolted for the front door of the shop—the same door, ironically enough, that he himself had locked up tight only a few hours earlier. Brutus, seeing an end to the game, leaped gleefully at his opponent and knocked him quite off his feet. Messrs. Pickett and Robinson moved in at once, the former hefting the apprentice to his feet with his arms held firmly behind his back, while the latter reached into the inside pocket of his coat and withdrew a thick wad of currency in varying denominations.

"I didn't steal it!" the young man insisted, his voice rising on a note of desperation. "My—my uncle died and left me a legacy. I thought I'd best lock it up for safe-keeping."

"In the middle of the night?" the linen-draper asked skeptically. "And where, pray, did you get a key to the safe?"

Seeing the apprentice had no intention of answering

this home question, Pickett hazarded a guess. "I expect it was during that time when your own key was missing," he told Mr. Robinson.

"But it was found not half an hour later," the man protested.

"It doesn't take long to press a key into warm wax— the side of a candle, for instance," Pickett pointed out. "Any locksmith can make a key from that impression."

"That was a month ago!" The linen-draper stared at his apprentice as if seeing him for the first time. "You must have been planning this for some time."

"I had to!" Andrew's voice rose on a note of hysteria. "You were going to make Miss Nancy marry that Brundy fellow!

"Oh, Andrew!" cried Miss Robinson, her voice choked with tears. "How could you?"

"Can't you see it was all for you?" Andrew pleaded with her. "I couldn't hope to marry you with nothing to settle on you, but how else was I to get the money? Your father would have had it back in the end, so what difference would it have made?"

" 'What difference,' Andrew?" Mr. Robinson shook his head sadly. "If you can't see it, there's no point in me trying to explain it to you."

"Shall I take him to Bow Street, sir?" Pickett offered.

Andrew, no doubt seeing the shadow of the gallows

looming before him, struggled to free himself. "Nancy, please! Don't let them—Nancy, I love you!"

"A strange sort of love, that steals from the loved one in order to win her," Pickett remarked.

"Much you know about it!" retorted Andrew, glaring over his shoulder at Pickett. "You'd probably tell me to settle for some female of my own station."

"No," Pickett said, not without sympathy. "No, I would never give another man advice I'm neither willing nor able to follow myself. Now, Mr. Robinson, if you'll unlock the door, I'll take this fellow off your hands."

"Don't think I'm not grateful, Mr. Pickett," the linen-draper said, "but I can't see him bound over for trial, not after he's lived under my roof since he was a lad. No, you can't stay," he told Andrew, whose face had lit up at the prospect of a reprieve. "You'll gather your things and go. And I'll watch you pack, for I've no doubt I'll find another roll of my money hidden among your possessions."

All the fight went out of Andrew, who no doubt knew better than to push his luck. He trudged slowly up the stairs with his master behind him, leaving Pickett alone with Miss Robinson.

"Thank you, Mr. Pickett," she said quietly, staring down at the candle in her hands with great concentration. "This is—hard—on all of us, but we do appreciate what you've done. If we seem less than grateful, it's because

Papa and I were both fond of Andrew. Even knowing what he did, it's difficult for me not to feel a bit sorry for him."

"And yet, pity is a poor reason to marry someone," Pickett pointed out.

She shook her head. "No, I could never do that, even if he hadn't—tell me, Mr. Pickett, will I—will I see you again?"

He did not have to ask why she should want to do so. "No, Miss Robinson," he said gently. "My work here is done."

"There are other reasons you might call," she said breathlessly.

"Miss Robinson—Nancy—I think you should know that I—I'm married."

"Married? Oh!" She pressed a hand to her bosom, as if he had plunged a dagger there. "I didn't know—you never said—"

"We are—estranged, my wife and I." It was all the explanation he felt capable of offering. "But I think I can reassure you on one matter, at least. You need have no fear of being forced into marriage with Mr. Brundy. He has no more desire to marry you than you have to marry him. I daresay the two of you together will be able to withstand any pressure that might be brought to bear." Privately, Pickett thought she might have done a great deal worse than Ethan Brundy, but the heart, after all, had its own reasons—as he had cause to know.

Since Mr. Robinson did not intend to prefer charges, Pickett judged it best to be gone before master and apprentice came back downstairs, in order to let them say their undoubtedly painful farewells in private. He bowed over Miss Robinson's hand and then let himself out the front door.

Outside, it was still dark but for the streetlamps casting pools of flickering light onto the pavement at intervals. He had no idea how late it might be; he'd lost all sense of time during the long wait for Andrew to make his move. Now he feared it was too early to report to Bow Street, yet too late to return to Drury Lane and seek his bed. And so he wandered aimlessly through the dark, quiet streets of Town until, inevitably, he found himself standing on a familiar corner in Curzon Street, gazing up at the dark windows of Number 22.

And quite suddenly, almost as if his thoughts had summoned her, one of the windows on the second story opened and a lady leaned out, her unbound hair spilling over the windowsill, pale in the moonlight.

Chapter 11

The End . . . Or Is It?

Julia awoke abruptly from the throes of nightmare, confused and disoriented at suddenly finding herself in her own bed, in her own room. In her dreams she had not been in her own house at all, but at Drury Lane Theatre, seated in a box overlooking the stage. Nor had she been alone, for John Pickett had been there, as well—not in the pit, where she had seen him once before, but in her own box, dressed as a gentleman (why was that particular aspect of the dream so painful to recall?) and looking every inch as if he belonged there. And suddenly, in the irrational manner of dreams, the theatre was ablaze, with great tongues of flame licking at the red velvet curtains of their box . . .

She'd awakened then, as was always the case when dreams turned dangerous. And yet it had all seemed so real that she could still smell the smoke, feel the heat scorching her lungs, choking her . . .

She threw back the covers, ran to the window, and

threw open the sash, then leaned out and breathed in great gulps of air—cold air, so cold that her breath appeared as small puffs of white, but wonderfully fresh after the suffocating black clouds of her nightmare.

Several minutes later, after her breathing had slowed down and her pounding heart had returned to normal, she bent her head and would have ducked back inside, had she not suddenly realized that she was not the only one awake at so late an hour. Across the street, a solitary figure stood in the pool of yellow light cast by the streetlamp on the corner, a tall, slender man dressed all in black. The lamplight was not sufficient for her to see his features clearly, but then, she had no need to; she recognized John Pickett at once, would have recognized him in much darker surroundings than these. Nor did she wonder at his presence; it seemed somehow natural that he should be there, as if he were part of the dream from which she had just awakened. Then an errant gust of wind blew her hair into her eyes, and when she'd brushed it back, he was gone. She closed the window and returned to bed, wondering if he'd ever really been there at all, or if that, too, had been a dream.

* * *

"You'll never believe who I encountered last night in St. James's Street," Lord Rupert Latham said, taking a teacup from Julia's hand and supplementing its contents from the flask in his coat pocket.

"Perhaps not, but I'm sure you intend to tell me anyway," Julia responded drily. She had not slept at all well the previous night, for her slumbers had been troubled by half-forgotten dreams that had ranged from the merely disturbing to the truly terrifying.

Ignoring this jibe, Lord Rupert leaned back complacently against the sofa cushions, the better to observe her discomfiture. "None other than your earnest young husband."

Julia's teacup clattered in its saucer. "Mr. Pickett?"

"Unless you have another husband I'm not aware of," said Lord Rupert, his eyebrows arching.

"How—how was he?" she asked, trying very hard to sound as if it didn't matter in the least.

"Half seas over, if you want to know the truth."

"Drunk?" she asked, startled. "He didn't—" She broke off abruptly. *He didn't look drunk*, she'd almost said. But it wouldn't do for Rupert to know about that midnight encounter, for a number of reasons—one of them being that she didn't know herself whether it had been real, or merely a product of her own half-dreaming imagination. "That is, he—he didn't ask after me, did he?"

"My dear Julia! Do you imagine that I make a habit of stopping in the street to bandy words with my intoxicated inferiors?"

"Not a habit, no," she retorted. "But I suspect that in the case of Mr. Pickett, you might make an exception."

"You know me too well, my dear," he conceded, chuckling. "That is why we would be so well-matched. As a matter of fact, yes, I did, er, exchange pleasantries with Mr. Pickett."

"By which you mean you said something hateful."

"Hateful? I?" Lord Rupert's expression was one of wounded innocence. "My dear Julia, do, pray, acquit me! I was merely emboldened by Mr. Pickett's, er, excesses to hope that they might be in honor, one might say, of the annulment of your marriage. But alas, he tells me my assumptions were premature."

Julia had ceased listening, for another thought had occurred to her. "Tell me, Rupert, was he—was he dressed all in black?"

Lord Rupert inclined his handsome head. "He was indeed, and it was this, along with his condition, that encouraged me to hope that he might be mourning the death of a dream."

It had been real, then. It warmed her heart to think of him standing in the street below, keeping watch over her like a knight of old protecting his lady. And no lady ever had a worthier, regardless of what Lord Rupert might say to the contrary. Nor was any knight more hardly used, she thought, suffering the now-familiar pang of guilt and shame at the demands placed on him by the annulment procedure. But according to her solicitor, the papers had already been filed, and it was merely a matter of waiting for the annulment to come before the ecclesiastical court.

And to hope, in the meantime, that she wasn't making the biggest mistake of her life.

Author's Note

Sharp-eyed readers will no doubt recognize Ethan Brundy, although this story takes place in December of 1808, eight (well, seven and a half) years before the events of his own book, which is set in the spring of 1816. Readers new to my books who want to know what happens when he *does*, in fact, meet the woman he wants to marry may read all about it in *The Weaver Takes a Wife*.

The seeds of his appearance here were first sown when I realized that, if they inhabited the same fictional "world," poor insecure John Pickett would actually be four years *older* than the self-assured Weaver, hero of what is probably the most popular novel I've ever written. It was interesting to think about, but a moot point, since I never expected them both to turn up in the same book.

Then John Pickett's newest case took him to a linen-draper's shop, and it seemed only natural that Ethan Brundy should turn up there, delivering a shipment of fabrics from his (or rather, his foster father's) warehouse. I had thought his would be no more than a cameo appearance, a sort of inside joke for people who had read *The Weaver Takes a Wife*; I should have known he would not be content with so insignificant a role!

About the Cover

The painting on the front of this book shows a 19th-century view of Drury Lane; I regret that I was unable to identify the artist of this particular work. The church whose steeple appears in the background is St. Mary-le-Strand, which is mentioned briefly in this story.

This exact streetscape appears again and again in sketches, paintings, and, later, photographs throughout the century, ranging in mood from charmingly picturesque to downright depressing as the century progressed. (To see a few of these images, check out www.pinterest.com/cobbsouth/waiting-game.) This particular painting was the only one that portrayed the street in wintertime, so I decided to use it even though it is evidently several decades later than the novella's setting of December 1808. How do I know? Because the double-gabled building in the right foreground was well-known as the Cock and Magpie pub at least as late as the 1840s; in this image, however, the distinctive sign between the second-floor windows has been taken down and/or painted over.

Sadly, this part of London no longer exists. The old Cock and Magpie, along with many other buildings, was demolished in 1900 to make room for the crescent-shaped street called Aldwych. In fact, the last time I was in London, my husband and I attended a stage production of the Fred Astaire classic *Top Hat* at the Aldwych Theatre, very close to where my fictional John Pickett would have lived.

About the Author

At the age of sixteen, Sheri Cobb South discovered Georgette Heyer, and came to the startling realization that she had been born into the wrong century. Although she doubtless would have been a chambermaid had she actually lived in Regency England, that didn't stop her from fantasizing about waltzing the night away in the arms of a handsome, wealthy, and titled gentleman.

Since Georgette Heyer died in 1974 and could not write any more Regencies, Ms. South came to the conclusion she would simply have to do it herself. In addition to her popular series of Regency mysteries featuring idealistic young Bow Street Runner John Pickett, she is the award-winning author of several Regency romances, including the critically acclaimed *The Weaver Takes a Wife*.

She loves to hear from readers, and invites them to visit her website, www.shericobbsouth.com; "Like" her author page at www.facebook.com/SheriCobbSouth; or email her via Cobbsouth@aol.com.

Made in the USA
Las Vegas, NV
11 April 2021

21023605R00074